HEMP

D'ANDRE BURKHALTER

DEDICATION

All praise be the glory to the GOD of My Being, Ross Smith, Jeremy Gums, Alexa Lisitza and Hemp Frankly.

CONTENTS

CHAPTER I

I woke up with a fully stuffed, dutched blunt on the marble white counter top, next to a Dom Perignon mimosa, with a note that read, "Thanks for the trip Daddy. Love, Your Lil' Baby."

Amazing right? But that's how those doctor types are — always on the go, even when they have a full paid vacation in a luxury hotel suite, beachside in the Bahamas. As my 8:30 alarm sets off, sending Future's "Percocet & Stripper Joint" vibrating all through the suite, I hopped out of bed, picked up my Dutch and Dom Perignon mimosa, walked out onto the balcony and started taking in the weather. After I finished my blunt and drink, I dashed inside the suite and hopped in the shower for a bit. After I came out, I immediately got dressed. I decided to wear something more comfortable so I threw on my Ralph Lauren sweatsuit, some shell toe Adidas, and a nice little Rolex. The valet came and brought the whip around, a chrome black Audi A5 Coupe — rental of course. I'm on vacation but when I get back I might have to cop one o' these. I gently popped the top, drove around a bit just to feel that Bahama breeze, and stopped in to eat at 1648 Bar & Grille, one of the finest restaurants on the island. I grabbed a couple of sliders, garlic grilled shrimp, and their version of spicy chicken.

I know what you're thinking. What line of work is he in to afford such a luxurious vacation? Well let's just say I'm a very successful cannabis connoisseur of sorts. See the whole illegal selling of weed was never my thing but when more states made it legal to sell, well then the conversation begins to change. And that's how I got interested in the multi-billion dollar marijuana industry. After graduating from the University of Chicago with a Bachelor's degree in business administration, I immediately packed my things and headed out of the Windy City to sunny California where the medical marijuana business was really taking off. Using some of my savings, I rented out a room for 12 months, got in contact with some growers and shop owners, and learned the business more and more.

Then, at 22 years old I moved to Seattle, WA where weed was just announced as legal for recreational use. This was a major game changer for me. Using the knowledge and skill I gained from working in California's medical marijuana industry and applying it to Seattle's recreational marijuana industry was a pretty easy transition. It seemed like the money just kept rolling in by the hundreds. My investors were pretty happy to see a nice return on their investments. Plus, some free ounces kept them a little more than happy.

After a couple of passion fruit drinks at 1648 Bar & Grille, I was ready to pay my bill. But not before one of the beautiful waiters approached me with some well needed small talk. Her overly friendly demeanor quickly let me know she was interested so I gave her my number and told her to call me if she wanted dinner and cocktails, on me of course — it's only the gentlemanly thing to do since I might bring her back for the causal night cap later.

Even though I took the weekend off for vacation, it's still all work in the tropics. I headed over to the crib of one of my top strain hunters, a multi-million dollar hustler from Queens, NY. See the job of a strain hunter is very cool, but it requires a high level of knowledge when it comes to the different global climates that certain strains grow in. This means strain hunters get to travel all over the world looking for the most potent marijuana strains and their seeds, either to sell to buyers like me or cross breed plants to get a more potent hybrid mix. Pulling up to my strain hunter's crib in a remote part of the islands, I peeped a brand new 2016 Aston Martin in the driveway — you know that new James Bond joint. I couldn't believe how long my boy's paper had gotten. I dipped out the whip, made my way to the beautiful crystal glass double doors, rang the hip-hop themed doorbell, and waited until this beautiful dark-skinned sister politely greeted and let me in. Walking past the two big white and gold sitting rooms into the massive sunk in living room, I saw my boy Ace chilling on his Milan-imported, black leather couch, just stuffing the money counter with hundred dollar US bills and fifty pound UK notes.

"Was up wit' it Ace?" I shout out.

He looks up, takes a fat ass blunt out his mouth, and says, "Shit my nigga Dre! What's good wit' it? Come on in here, cop a squat, and come roll you up some o' this Jamaican good good."

Sinking into the fine leather black couch, I took out a pack of chocolate Dutches, cracked them open, and began to roll some Jamaican premium gas. The beautiful dark-skinned sister from before asked if I would like anything. I politely told her, "Some orange juice." Then, me and Ace got straight to discussing business. As I sipped my orange drink and took slow hard hits of the marijuana smoke, he began to strike a deal with me — 5,000 seeds straight out of the amazon, plus 10 pounds of this bomb ass Jamaican shit for 50 bands.

"My nigga Ace, always coming through with the hookup," I said.

He replied,"Dre you already know how we get down fam'. I've been fuckin' wit' you since those university days."

"You right, you right. You've been a stand up dude since day one," I said.

He took out his e-card reader and I pull out my black card from a handmade leather wallet I got from a street vendor in Bristol, UK. I know this isn't how normal drug dealers do business. You were probably expecting the usual 100K, all hundreds, in a Louis V duffle bag or black leather brief case with a strap, conveniently tucked in my backside. But this isn't one of those gangster movies and I'm not a drug dealer. I'm a business man and this is a multi-billion dollar industry I'm apart of; I take my money and business very seriously.

I swipe my card and finish up our business. Ace told me everything will be shipped by an Uber styled speedboat shipping service he uses for special business like this. We celebrated our business transaction by cracking open a bottle of Ace of Spades and begun pouring up. We toasted our crystal glasses and rocked to our own soundtrack.

"Ace you stay pouring up the golden bottles each time I shop with you," I said.

"Of course. You already know — that's why they call me Ace boy," he expressed.

We both busted out in laughter, kicking around a couple o' jokes, talking good shit. You already know, just chilling, smoking and making money while on vacation. God I love my life. An unknown number began to ring my phone. I automatically knew who it was, seeing that I only gave my number to one person today. I told Ace to hold on and then picked up the phone. "Yo was up Ms. Waiter?" I said jokingly.

"Ha Ha, I see you like to make jokes American boy," she replied.

"You already know. So what's up? Are we still on for tonight?" I said.

"Yes. I would like to still go out. Where do you want me to meet you?" she asked.

"Meet me at my hotel. Call me when you get there so I can meet you in the lobby," I replied.

She said, "Ok I'll call when en route." Then we hung up.

"Yo Ace, thanks for the blunts and fine champagne but I have to dip. There's a fine little dark-skinned island sister waiting for me back at the hotel," I stated.

"Shit, say no more. It's always a pleasure doing business with you Dre," he said.

"You already know," I replied.

Then we dapped hands and the fine dark-skinned sister from before politely showed me out. I stepped out and immediately felt the cool Bahama breeze mixed with the tropical heat. I took out my Gucci sunglasses, put them on, walked over to the car, got in, took one of the blunts I rolled at Ace's crib, sparked it, turned on some Ricky Rozay — you know, my favorite Renzal album, "Black Market" of course. I started up the car and just like that, I was gone and onto other business/pleasure. Forty minutes later, I arrived at the hotel. I stepped out the whip, let the valet do his job, entered into the big lobby of the hotel, made my way to the suite, got undressed, hopped in the shower, and after my warm, sauna-like shower, threw on a white Ralph Lauren sweat suit, and patiently waited for my seven o'clock.

Exactly at seven o'clock, I started to hear a knock. I opened the door and there stood a slim, thick, honey brown, dread head sister. It was the waiter from earlier. She stepped in, took off her flats, and proceeded outside to the patio, and onto the beach where I had a nice candle lit dinner set up. Pink and orange hues really set the mood as the sun rested on the crystal blue Bahamian beach shore. The hotels chef really came through with a traditional Bahamian meal that consented of jerk chicken, fresh lobster tail, shrimp, and yellow rice, nicely accommodated with a bottle of Century White wine. A couple of good conversations and glasses of white wine later, we were ready to head back inside my suite. After all, I couldn't be up all night. I had to catch my eleven a.m. flight back to Seattle, WA.

At dusk the next morning, I woke up to a perfectly rolled strawberry swisher sweet on the coffee table, right next to a glass of orange juice and a strawberry kiwi smoothie. Man this hotel really took care of a brother. I let Wiz Khalifa's song "Mary 3x" play though my Beats Pill as I finished my blunt and smoothie. I got undressed, then headed to the shower.

During my steaming hot shower, I had the time to reminisce about the events that took place last night. Damn shorty could of easily been the best I ever had while on one of my trips to the Bahamas, but you know how it goes. I couldn't let her stay the night so I called her an Uber after we finished our business.

Thirty minutes later, I stepped out the shower, dried off, walked into my suite, grabbed my blue Versace silk boxers, Ralph Lauren tee, and matching Ralph Lauren socks from out of my luggage. The night before, I laid out and ironed my navy blue Zara slacks and white Ralph Lauren shirt. I checked the weather report on my phone and it said by the time I get back to Seattle, it'll be windy, cloudy and a forty percent chance of rain. So I decided to throw on my matching navy Zara blazer. After I threw on my navy suede Ferragamo belt and gold oyster bezel Rolex, I packed all my luggage, took it out in the hallway for the bell hop to take it to the rental, grabbed my Fendi laptop case and keys, made my way out the front door. After locking it, I walked to the elevator, rode it down to the lobby, turned in my room key at the front desk and waited for valet to pull the car around. Finally, the valet came around with the whip. I quickly hopped in and sped off.

Fuck, I'm always late for my flights but luckily Grand Bahama International Airport was only twenty-five minutes away from the hotel. Plus, I had first class tickets so everything was going to be fast anyway. Exactly twenty-five minutes later, I was at the airport. I took my luggage out the trunk, turned in the rental, then quickly made my way inside the airport. I got my luggage checked in quite fast so I was even able to grab something eat. Thank god for first class. Relaxing in the first class waiting area, I just day dreamed to myself about how hard I had worked to get to the spot I'm in today. I never would have achieved this level of success if I hadn't believed in myself. But not too long into self-reflecting on my life, my flight was already being called. I boarded along with first class, took my seat by the window of course, took out a special little brownie I had, ate it, and patiently waited until the plane ascended into the sky.

CHAPTER II

A couple of hours later, I woke up to the pilot's voice instructing us to turn off all electronic devices and to buckle our seat belts. Finally we made it to Seattle. Whenever I'm on a long plane ride, I always eat a weed brownie. It puts me straight to sleep so I won't be so bored on six to nine hour flights. The pilot

O.K.'d us to unbuckle our seat belts and exit. I grabbed my Fendi laptop case from the carry-on luggage compartment above, made my way to the exit, and strolled onto the terminal. A moment later, I arrived at baggage claim, grabbed my luggage and departed the Seattle-Tacoma International Airport. I then went to the parking garage to pick up my whip, a 2016 Jaguar F-Type convertible that I copped for my twenty-fifth birthday last June. A whole weekend of rain showers had it looking *too* clean. I pulled out the parking garage, headed toward the expressway and skated onto the I-5 connecter. I rode that out for fourteen quick minutes, hopped on the I-90 connecter and then exited onto MLK Parkway. Nine minutes later I pulled into my garage.

Finally home. As I unbuckled my seat belt, my phone began to ring, sending Rick Ross's "Diced Pineapples" vibrating all through my car. I gave some of my associates specific ringtones so I didn't need to look at my phone to know who it was.

"Yo wassup Niniette! You know I just touched back down in the city—what's up with you?" I questioned.

"I can see, you're always posting everything for the 'gram but I want to discuss some business with you. Can you meet me for lunch at IL Fornaio's in thirty minutes?" she said.

"Yea I'll definitely be there. I'll text you when I'm close," I stated.

"Alright Dre, see you then," she said.

Then we both hung up. Niniette Jackson was a fine ass real estate agent from Atlanta, GA. After I started making real money in this business, I hit her up about this crib and we closed the deal for a smooth $2.8 million dollars. After the deal was done, I invited her out to celebrate and by the end of the night we had some bomb ass accidental sex. Then we kept having bomb ass accidental sex until we decided to just be friends that like to have accidental sex from time to time. I like to reminisce on those times, especially when I'm sitting in my garage.

After wrapping up my phone conversation I grabbed my Fendi laptop case and luggage from the back seat and headed

11

inside my 5,053 square foot, three bedroom, four bathroom home, accommodated with an indoor pool that I barely use, a chefs' kitchen that I'm always cooking something in, and a secret garden where I grow vegetables, fruits and some of my favorite strains. Yeah this house really fits my needs.

I headed past the main living room, up the stairs, and all the way to the master bedroom. I decided to take a shower and get dressed for my business date so I immediately undressed, started my shower, got my Beats Pill out my luggage, and begun to play Erykah Badu's radio station on Pandora as I decided on what to wear. Since the rain had stopped, I laid out a grey Nike tech sweat suit on my California king size bed, then hopped in my warm shower and washed up for a good fifteen minutes. I dried off, walked over to my boxer drawer, picked out some all white Tommy Hilfiger joints, then began to get dressed. I walked over to my spacious walk in closet, went to my sneaker section, and grabbed some all cocaine white high top Air Force ones, as well as a Lexington sliver tone Michael Kors watch from my Louis Vuitton watch case. I lightly sprinkled on some Ralph Lauren cologne and just like that, I was ready for my business date at IL Fornaio's inside of Pacific Place shopping mall.

I was already running three minutes late, so I quickly made my way down stairs to the main living room, and into the garage. I started up the whip and then dashed out of the garage. Luckily Pacific Place shopping mall was only fifteen minutes away so I shot shorty a text and let her know I was in route. Fifteen minutes later, I was pulling into the parking garage of Pacific Place shopping mall. I paid the ten dollar parking fee for three hours. *Three hours… shit, a nigga might as well grab some fresh shit while I'm here,* I thought to myself.

After paying my fee and parking my car, I decided to take the street entrance inside the mall. So I walked out of the parking garage, down the street, turned the corner, then entered into the mall. While walking through Pacific Place shopping mall, I noticed there weren't a lot of people. But then again it was a Monday afternoon and I hate crowded malls anyway, so why was I complaining? IL Fornaio's was my favorite Italian restaurant in the whole metropolitan of Seattle. A reservation was required since they were always packed. I already knew I was about to hear Niniette's mouth about my tardiness. I walked into Il Fornaio's and I saw Niniette waving me over. All I could think was: *AWW HELL here we go!*

Walking over to the ornately decorated white cloth table, I automatically felt Niniette's angry but loving energy.

"DRE!" she said excitedly as she stood up and hugged me.

"Wassup baby girl?" I said smoothly hoping she didn't cuss me out in front of all these white people.

"Dre, what the fuck is your problem? Always late and shit — you're lucky I'm trying to keep it classy by not smacking the shit out of you in front of these good white folk," she stated.

"Girl calm down," I said jokingly as we both began to sit down.

The waiter came over and asked if we were ready to order. I politely waited for Niniette to order her food. Then, I ordered lemonade and my favorite dish, the "Linguine Mare Chiaro." It consisted of thin flat pasta with clams, mussels, prawns, and scallops, seasoned with tomatoes, crushed red pepper, and white wine. After taking down our orders, the waiter said he would be right back with our drinks. So I turned my attention back to Niniette and asked her what exactly she wanted to discuss.

"Ok, so check this out," she smoothly stated. "There are four fat ass cribs down in Atlanta that I want you to go half and half with me on. The total would be about a hundred fifty thousand each," she concluded with a serious tone. A few more in depth conversations later and I agreed to do the deal.

"Damn Niniette, You're always so persistent," I stated.

"Nigga, of course. And if my logic didn't work, then I was probably going to have to get you up outta here nice and drunk, take you to my play room, and do that thing you always like with the handcuffs," she jokingly said.

"Whatever nigga," I playfully said. Then, I threw a hundred-dollar bill on the table to take care of lunch. "Alright Niniette, it's been real fucking with you, but a nigga has to bounce. Have a great rest of the day," I sincerely said.

"Ok Dre. Me, you and Atlanta in four weeks," she stated and I nodded in agreement.

After walking out of IL Foranio's with a slightly stuffed stomach from their amazing Italian food, I decided to do some light ballin', so I hit up one of my favorite clothing stores inside the mall called "Club Monaco." Sometimes Club Monaco has great clothes for my style, especially during this cold ass fall season. I immediately saw this dope ass varsity jacket in my size, so I tired it on and looked in the mirror. *Damn, I could get so many hoes in this joint,* I thought to myself. I approached the checkout register and was frozen in my steps by how beautiful the cashier was. I began to get into my mac daddy mode, checked my breath, and then walked up to the register like I was about to buy the store. She politely greeted me and I automatically started running game.

"I'm fine, thanks for asking. How are you?" I flirtatiously asked.

"I've been better but I can't wait to get off work. I'm so tired," she said dreadfully.

"Poor thing, but I've definitely been there before. Can I ask you a question?" I said.

"Sure. You're the one paying five hundred dollars for a jacket, so I guess I'll give you slight conversation," she jokingly said.

"What do you do during the day?" I questioned.

"I'm currently a senior at Seattle Pacific University," she said.

"That's wassup. What's your major?" I questioned.

"I'm majoring in creative writing. I'm sort of a poet with my words," she said with a shy smile.

"Oh word? I love poetry. We should get together so I can read your work," I smoothly said.

"Sure, Mr. Money man. I would love that," she said with a smile. She wrote her number on my receipt and just like that I snatched up another one.

After leaving Pacific Place Mall, I decided to stop by my favorite chicken spot, Ezell's Famous Chicken, to pick up some of their good ass buffalo tenders, Cajun fries, and a couple of pieces from their famous chicken selection. I arrived back to the crib with a nice box of freshly fried chicken and Cajun fries and was ready for my nightly smoke session. I went upstairs to the master bedroom, stepped into my walk-in closet, and grabbed a jar of Purple OG Kush, a grinder, and a king sized pre-coned Raw rolling paper. I then began to stuff my grinder. Nightly smoke sessions always consisted of strong indica strains that put me straight to sleep. Since I was stuffing my pre-coned Raw joint with this dank ass bud, I decided to turn on some entertainment. I'm not much of a cable watcher so I just turned on my big ass 4K resolution flat screen, opened up my YouTube app, and watched one of my favorite people, Kevin Gates, interview with The Breakfast Club. Twenty minutes later, I was already high as fuck and dying laughing from this Kevin Gates interview. *Man this nigga is a five-star luxury trip. Boy, I tell you,* I thought to myself. I checked the time. "Oh shit it's 11:30 p.m. already. Shit, I gotta hit the sheets." I decided to just crash on the couch with my high ass, so I put out my joint, turned off the T.V, and laid down until I was in deep peaceful sleep.

At sunrise, I began to open my eyes and immediately grabbed my phone from the coffee table to check the time. "It's eight o'clock, FUCK!" I was supposed to be at the warehouse two hours ago but fuck it when you're the boss you can afford to be late. I wasn't doing anything special anyway, other than popping up and making sure everything is everything. Immediately, I dashed upstairs for a quick shower and got dressed faster than usual. I felt like being on my 80's RUN DMC type swag, so I just threw on an all-black Adidas sweat suit with the clean white and black Adidas. I added a nice gold Cartier watch for a little flavor.

15

No matter how late I am, I never miss my morning smoke session or breakfast. Shit, if I'm late for a flight, I will reschedule it just to smoke and eat. I don't play about my mornings, seeing as I'm not much of a morning person anyway.

Sour Diesel was my strain of choice for the morning and since I was running late I just grabbed a wine Dutch, cracked it open, dumped the tobacco, then begin to roll this sour goodness as I warmed up some of that bomb ass chicken I had last night. While walking outside to my villa-like terrace with my blunt of Sour D and a half eaten box of fried chicken, I began to do some self-reflecting on my life. Fuck, I honestly don't know where I would be in life if I didn't believe in myself. That was the most important part to my success — believing in my talents and abilities. While taking long hits of the good Sour Diesel, my phone began to ring. Judging by the mellow ring tone, I immediately knew who it was. "Yo John, wassup man how are you?" I said.

"Shit, I'm good. I just wanted to check up with you," he replied.

"Man you know how I'm always on the clock, just in different time zones, trying to make this paper," I said.

"Shit nigga, I hear that but yo check this out. Are you busy today?" he questioned.

"Naw, nothing more than the usual. Just hitting the warehouse up and making sure everything is everything. Why, wassup?" I asked curiously.

"Alright when you get back from the warehouse, shoot me a text and I'm going to come scoop you up," he said.

"Alright, say no more. I got you," I said and then hung up.

Shit, a nigga was still slick tired but duty called. So after I finished my blunt and leftover fried chicken, I locked up, turned on the alarm, then dipped out in the Jag and was on my way to the warehouse to check on my plants, bud, and other cannabis products. As I pulled up to my warehouse, I wondered what the homie had to scoop me up for. "Oh well, fuck it. Hopefully he buys lunch cause I'm not trying to spend any bread today," I thought. One of my head growers came out to greet me as I got out the car. "Wassup Dre? Everything has been on the up and up. We've moved almost half of that Jamaican shit you got from the Bahamas," he said.

"God damn! We've moved that much? I just got back yesterday!" I said in amazement.

"Aye man, I was surprised too but can you really be surprised, though?" he stated.

"Hell yea, what you mean?" I questioned.

"Nigga you know your connects always come through. Plus, Seattle is in need of that good tropic gas," he factually stated.

"Shit my nigga, you ain' never lied. By the time these Jamaican seeds finish their grow cycle, I'll have successfully made another million," I happily said.

"You already know," he said.

Then we entered my 12,400 square feet warehouse that I payed almost 900K for. Me and my boys converted it into four sections — flowing, cloning, extracts and trimming. Whenever I check in at the warehouse, I'm just usually checking to make sure all my plants are being grown properly and that the temperatures for all sections are correct. After walking through the warehouse and checking everything, I made my way out and shot my homie a text so he could meet me at my crib. Fifteen minutes later, I pulled up to my homie John parked on the curb. I rolled down the window and told him to sit tight while I park the whip in the garage. I parked my Jag in the garage, hopped out, let the garage down, then walked out to the curb and into my nigga John's 2014 BMW M3.

John owned a weed shop forty minutes away from me. He was one of my first clients and now a very good friend. Twenty minutes later, we pulled up to Evergreen Speedway. "Oh shit, what are we doing here? We better not be doing what I think we are about to do!" I happily stated.

We hopped out his whip after he parked it, entered through the gates, and all I saw was two cars — a black BMW I8 and a red Porsche 917. "Damn John! you rented out Evergreen Speedway just for us to race?" I asked while surprised.

"Hell yeah but not for nothing though. I got 5K that you can't beat me in a five lap race," he stated frankly.

"Shit nigga, you better put your money where your mouth is. I'm game for a challenge," I stated with all seriousness.

"Alright, choose your pick while I roll up real quick," he said.

"Nigga, I'm all for a good smoke session but really, right now?" I asked jokingly.

"Young nigga, I've been doing this since ninety-five. I got this. You just better have my money," he said.

"Whatever, old head," I responded. We busted out laughing.

After a couple of hits from his blunt, I jumped in the Porsche 917 and he hopped in the BMW I8. "Alright, you ready young nigga?" he teased while revving the engine.

"Shit let's get it," I yelled.

Then the man in the high raise box waved the flag and just like that we were off. With a hundred miles on the dash I quickly took the lead and won lap one, but John was right behind me cutting sharp turns on some "Tokyo Drift" shit. However, that didn't phase me seeing as though I had won laps two and three. On lap four, John was really on my shit but I kept swerving right to left so he couldn't get in front of me. I won lap four and felt confident in my soon-to-be victory. I even thought about how I was going to spend that 5K, but out of nowhere this nigga was neck to neck with me. While a couple of feet from the finish line, this nigga looked at me, smiled high as fuck, then kicked that bitch into another gear and won the race. "GOD DAMN FUCK—I WASN'T TRYING TO SPEND ANY MONEY TODAY!"

"YEA YOUNG NIGGA YOU WERE POPPING ALL THAT GOOD SHIT A MINUTE AGO. NOW RUN ME MY MONEY," he said high as hell while getting out the car.

"Fuck you John," I said while taking out my checkbook and writing his punk ass five thousand dollars.

"Aww young nigga, don't get in your feelings. I got some wings and good bud for us to smoke while we chop it up about some business," he said.

"Shit, at least you feedin' a nigga and frying me up," I said.

We headed over to the stands where there were two boxes of chicken and 3.5 grams of some purp. "Damn John, these are some good ass hot wings!" I said while he rolled up three fat ass blunts of the purp. He sparked one blunt to start off the rotation then immediately got straight to business.

"So this is what I really came to holler at you about. There's this cigar shop where they hand roll some of the best cigars in the world and I wanted to know if you would like to roll with me over there in three weeks," he said.

"Where is this cigar shop?" I asked.

"Granada, Nicaragua," he said.

"Oh shit. Word nigga, did you have to ask? Hell yeah! Where are we going to be staying at?" I questioned with excitement.

"Mukul Beach & Spa Resort," he said.

"Shit, say no more. You already know I'm fucking with it. Just text me the details," I said. We kicked it for another good thirty minutes eating good, smoking better, and just enjoying the fruits of our hard labor. But soon into relaxing, I got a text asking, "Do you want to hang out tonight?" I immediately knew who it was—that beautiful, honey brown shorty from the mall. I texted her back with "Sure, dinner at my place. Asian?" She texted back, "Sounds great. See you later on." I told the homie John that I had to dip in order to prepare for my dinner date, so we finished the last blunt, hopped back in his whip, and took off back to my crib.

Soon as John dropped me off at my spot I let up the garage, hopped in the whip, and headed to Uwajimaya Asian supermarket to pick up ingredients for tonight's dinner — Salmon Kasuzuke. Fifteen minutes later, I pulled back up to the crib, pulled into the garage, and headed upstairs to my chef-style kitchen to prep the salmon and vegetables. Precisely at seven o'clock, I hear a knock at my door. Perfect timing as dinner was almost ready. "Damn Mr. Money man. Whatever you have cooking smells amazing," she jokingly said.

"Naw shorty. Whatever fragrance you're wearing smells amazing," I said with a smile.

"Thanks, but it's nothing fancy. Just some perfume from Victoria Secret," she said while trying to play it cool.

I told her to make herself comfortable in the main living room while I prep our plates. Before I brought out our plates, I lit a couple of strawberry candles and set my Beats Pill at a nice volume so Jill Scott's soulful voice could set the mood.

"I'm feeling this vibe, Dre. I love Jill," she said.

"Of course. Who doesn't?" I said while bringing our plates out.

After setting our plates in the dining room, I grabbed a bottle of red wine from my wine cellar in the kitchen and two grams of Chronic to enhance our taste buds. First, we smoked. Then we began to eat, drink and just enjoy our energies mixing into a super good vibe. After we finished dinner, still high as hell and now a little tipsy, we went upstairs to my room where she discovered my private library. "Hill Harper's Letter To A Young Brother. Hmm very interesting," she said curiously.

"Yea I got that book when I was a teenager. I read it every year," I said.

She took off her shoes and shirt and jumped in my bed. As I took off my shirt and climbed into bed, I asked her, "Would you

20

like to read to me?" She nodded, then laid her head on my chest and began to read to me. Her voice was so sweet, but passionate. Before I knew it, I had dozed off. Daybreak woke me up the following morning and I noticed a glass of orange juice with a kiwi wedge on my coffee table a note that read, "Good morning, Dre. I wish I could have stayed the night, but I had to get back to my dorm. I had a great time last night. Hopefully we can do it again. Love Christine."

Damn, I thought. *Isn't that about a bitch. We didn't even fuck.* But I always respect a woman that doesn't let me hit on the first date. It makes them more attractive. Three weeks later I was packing luggage for my five day trip to Nicaragua and then a few days in Atlanta. It seemed like time just flew by.

Every luxury that I have in life is a straight reflection of the work I put in to get it. Without working smarter and being dedicated and disciplined to my self and my goals, none of this shit would be possible, I thought in self-reflection.

I needed a blunt, so I went to my walk in closet, grabbed a jar of some Sour Kush and a single wine Dutch, then proceeded to stuff 2.5 grams in my blunt. After finishing my fat ass blunt, I took my luggage downstairs to the garage and put it in the trunk of my car. Then, I hopped in the shower for a good fifteen minutes, jumped out and threw on a white & black Zara polo shirt with some white Zara chino shorts, Tom Ford belt, and Giuseppe loafers, and then locked up. I hopped in the car and drove to Seattle-Tacoma International airport. After parking my car in the airport parking garage, I got my luggage checked in, which was a pretty fast process since John got us first class tickets. And speaking of a "stoner," there was John, patiently waiting for our flight to be called while reading a newspaper. Man, I swear this dude was so old school.

"Wassup, old head?" I said jokingly.

We dapped up. "Shit, nothing young nigga. How are you? And did you bring the cookies?" he asked.

"Nigga, do you have to ask? I'm not about to be awake for ten hours on a plane. I need to be passed out high," I stated.

"Alright, say no more," he said as they announced first class to board. John and I both took our seats then ate three weed cookies that were made with the strain God's Gift, which is already a powerful indica for sleeping when you smoke it. Eating it just intensifies the effect, so you know we were about to be gone until we touched down in Managua, Nicaragua.

CHAPTER III

Thirty minutes before we landed I woke up hungry as hell, still well rested thanks to those weed cookies. Reaching in my pocket I grabbed my phone, checked the time, then plugged in my headphones and begun to go to my Tidal music app and played my favorite song "Drippin'" off Future's mixtape "Purple Reign." The song meant a lot to me, before all these millions I use to be a broke ass nigga on the south side of Chicago. Girls use to diss me just because I wasn't on the block risking my life or freedom, getting to that paper. Now those same girls want a taste of the high life, isn't that a bitch? But I'm drippin' on them now, I wonder how they love that?

I pressed the button above me to call over the flight attendant so she could get a brother some chips and water. With twenty minutes until we touchdown in Managua, Nicaragua I was starting to sober up. Fifteen minutes later and the pilot comes over the intercom instructing us to turn off all electronic devices as we were preparing to land. The landing was so rough John woke up "What the fuck is going on, damn a nigga is trying to sleep!" he grumpily said.

"Nigga were here now" I jokingly said. Then we unbuckled our seat belts, got all of our carry on shit proceeded down terminal, then to baggage claim and then I waited outside Augusto C. Sandino International Airport while John went to go pick up a rental. This nigga John comes around the corner with a 2015 Mercedes Benz E- Class Cabriolet.

"God damn nigga I like your style, this shit is stupid clean!"
I stated.

"Hell yeah I was thinking about coping one of these joints
anyway," he said while dropping the top.

After loading our luggage in the trunk we immediately
peeled off since we had a long two hour drive to Mukul Beach &
Spa Resort. John brought a bunch of THC capsules, which are just
a THC extract pressed into capsules, they get you super fucked up;
it's like the same thing as smoking five blunts of good gas. Under
the influence of the THC pills, the Nicaraguan wild life looked so
amazing. Parrots, toucans and hummingbirds provided natural
music along with color. Sloths hanging in the highest of trees made
me feel relaxed and clam. Being in the presence of colorful, natural
lands high as hell with the top of a very fast and luxurious car
dropped really had me thinking about what's really important in
life. Don't get me wrong I love fancy shit, I mean why wouldn't I
when growing up it was a struggle just to keep food in the house.
Ultimately I thank those humble beginnings, because the hard
struggle inspired the hard hustle.

An hour later we pulled up to the entrance of the resort. It
was so beautiful, picture a bunch of open beach villas facing the
Pacific Ocean. Each of them with there own private pools. You
could even smell the freshness from the crystal blue ocean in the
atmosphere. Our rooms were very open, there was only one wall
and three thick curtains. John and I really wanted to go surfing
before nightfall so we got showered up. After my open shower I
threw on some black Ralph Lauren gym shorts with a Ralph
Lauren wife beater. I met up with John under the huge straw and
tree pavilion. We sat in the two chairs that overlooked the private
pool, palm trees and ocean. To my surprise this nigga takes out
fourteen grams of some very everest green looking shit.

"When and where did you cop some bud from?!" I
questioned.

"Nigga now you know I have mad connections around the
world" he expressed with a smirk.

"Shit whatever nigga lets smoke!" I happily replied.

He took out a pack of wine Dutch masters, handed me one,
and then we began stuffing our blunts with the everest green
Nicaraguan bud. Sunset, was approaching quite fast so we put out

our blunts and made our way to the surf board rental shop. I was looking so clean with my blue and white wetsuit with the blue and white surfboard to match. I just had to get a picture for the 'gram.

"What the fuck, nigga I know your not doing that Instagram shit again" John questioned while laughing.

"Nigga fuck you, it's 2016 not 1995; this is how you get the hoes now a days, keep up with the times old man," I jokingly replied as we exited out the shop.

The waves were so gentle to coast on but once you crashed you could feel the roughness of the Pacific ocean. It felt so good to feel the misty cool breeze hit my face as I glided through waves. This nigga John kept falling and shit with his high ass. My euphoric state allowed me to just surf smoothly as if I've been doing this for years. The sun was starting to fall as we wrapped up surfing for the day. John went to go turn in our wet suits and surf boards while I made the call to the resort so there chef could cook us some dinner. We felt like eating some good chicken so I told them to whip us up a twenty piece. Ten hot, extra wet and ten lemon pepper with garlic butter fries and a kiwi strawberry smoothie with a splash of Henny. Once John came back we both decided to take a shower and meet back up under the pavilion.

After my shower I felt so relaxed and just at peace. I guess this is how the Central American atmosphere makes you feel. John, was already under the pavilion sitting by the table that was directly centered under the tree bark chandelier, rolling some of that Nicaraguan bud he had from earlier. I took a seat in front of him and began rolling up a couple of fat ass blunts for myself. A waiter came by and delivered our wings, fries and smoothie. We politely tipped him fifty dollars each then got straight to smoking, eating, and talking about the plans for tomorrow.

"What's the move for tomorrow John? Are we going to that cigar shop?" I questioned while tearing up my twenty piece.

"First of all slow your black ass down, nigga; I mean like damn, you're over here going in on this chicken!" he jokingly expressed.

"Nigga shut up this shit is A1!" I replied while laughing.

"Nigga you ain't never lied, this shit is hittin' but I'm thinking about hitting up the cigar shop the day after tomorrow," he replied.

"Alright bet, that gives me a day to see what there spa treatment is about," I expressed.

"I feel you, just make sure you schedule a morning appointment. We're going on a boat ride around the Pacific coast and then fishing," he stated.

"Alright cool, now I have a reason to bust out my Ralph Lauren bucket hat," I happily replied.

"See that's some young nigga shit. Like damn, do you have to be fresh everywhere you go," he jokingly expressed while taking a smooth hit of the weed smoke.

"First of all, if you don't get your LL Cool Jay smooth smoking ass the fuck out of here, and I know this isn't coming from the same nigga that has on a pair of Gucci flip-flops. Nigga who you think you are, Future?" I jokingly replied, while coughing from the weed smoke.

"See look at you, young nigga over here about to die coughing your lungs out — baby ass smoker. And fuck you, I have a bunch of investments that are doing quite well so I can afford to splurge," he replied.

"Well old head, you and I both," I replied.

"Word what investments you got?" he questioned.

"Shit, I put some money in the stock market, U.S government bonds and now my realtor Niniette is about to get me set up in the real estate game," I replied.

"Oh yeah, you did tell me about that," he stated as we both finished our twenty piece, fries, smoothie and blunts.

"Alright young nigga, an old nigga has to get some rest. I'll catch up with you morning," he expressed with a yawn. "Meet me on the beach at day break for breakfast," he tiredly stated.

"Alright old nigga, don't throw your hip out of place sleeping," I jokingly replied as we went to our rooms to catch some sleep.

My eyes opened exactly at day break the next morning. I hopped up out of bed and then opened one of the curtains. *GOD DAMN IT'S HOT!* I thought to myself as I walked out on the beach to meet John for breakfast. "Yo, wassup" I tiredly expressed as we dapped hands.

"Nothing much, just waiting on your late ass," he replied.

"I already ordered our breakfast it should be on the way in ten minutes," he stated as he took out some weed and two Wiz Khalifa rolling papers. We begin two roll up and smoke up as we waited for our order.

"Yo John, you never told me — what you got going on today?" I questioned while sparking my joint.

"Shit, well I'm about to be on my Tiger Woods shit today," he stated. "This resort has a beautiful eighteen hole golf course."

"Nigga you ain't shit in golf, fake Tiger Woods lookin' ass nigga!"I jokingly responded, while hitting my joint.

"See, that is what's wrong with you young niggas always hating" he expressed.

"Bet you won't put a stack on a nine hole game" he seriously stated.

"Nigga I already lost 5K to you. Fuck it, I'm that nigga in golf so it's whatever," I replied.

"Say less, your loss not mine," he stated.

"I don't know what I'm going to spend your thousand on, should I get one of my hoes a new Prada bag or just cash out on some new suits?" he expressed in deep thought.

Finally our food had arrived. When your high, time goes by so slow. "Oh shit, John you ordered my favorite scrambled eggs with a fillet of wild salmon, a tall glass of orange juice, and a strawberry smoothie?" I stated in astonishment.

"Nigga now you know, I know you," he said.

"True, true," I said while immediately attacking my food.

"See here you go eating like a fucking savage!" he jokingly stated.

"I know right, just how your shorty likes it," I jokingly replied, as we busted out in laughter.

"Nigga you funny as hell but I'm about to go shower up and change," he stated.

"Me too" I stated.

"Alright cool meet me under the pavilion at twelve o'clock, don't be late. I'm not running on C.P.T!" he sternly stated.

"Say no more, and I'm always fifteen to thirty minutes late," I stated.

"Why?" he questioned.

"'Cause I'm a boss," I playfully stated.

"Well see what happens if you come late, your boss ass can surely get left," he half jokingly, half seriously expressed.

"Shut the fuck up, I'll be there nigga!" I jokingly responded, as we started busting out into more laughter. As John and I departed from breakfast on the beach I thought about what I was going to wear. Maybe I should bust out the Puma sweat suit, no, it's to hot for that shit. You know what, I'm just going to keep it simple. Some black H&M cargo shorts, white H&M v-neck, black Ralph Lauren bucket, black Versace slides and the black Versace socks to match should be dope. *Hell yeah that sounds like a plan*, I thought to myself while starting up my shower.

The showers at Mukal Beach & Spa Resort are so relaxing. I might have to make some renovations to my bathroom, I thought to myself as I stepped out the shower and got dressed. After getting dressed, I made my way out out my room onto the beach and right up to the spa suites. Upon my arrival I was escorted by this fine ass Hispanic masseuse. She walked me through the private entry garden for the foot bath ritual. Which basically is where they have your feet soak in an herbal bath. They wash and scrub your feet, which is always awkward for me. The only person I let wash and scrub my dirty ass feet is Niniette. She loves to pamper me, just as much as I do her. Next they took me to the one of their private spa suites, called the healing hut. A brother needs some spiritual healing before I leave Nicaragua to go do some business in Atlanta with Niniette crazy ass.

"Oh my god!" I expressed to myself. This masseuse is really relaxing my muscles, with this Indian herbal scrub. Even though this treatment is suppose to relax my muscles, rid my body of toxins, and reduce stress, it's like I can literately feel all those things happening at once. For the final part of my spa treatment I was escorted back to the spa garden to sit comfortably in there plunge pool. It's set to heat up then cool down to help circulate blood flow, get rid of more toxins, and cleanse the skin.

Being in that plunge pool for a good hour surely had me reminiscing. I remember making my first million and just blasting "Finally Rich" by Chief Keef. That day was the best day of my life. I bought three different BMW's, which I ended up selling. Then I got a fully furnished, huge four room townhouse. I just sat in the living and cried so hard, thinking, *finally, I had accomplished great success.* Then later on that night I hit up my boys and partied too fuckin' hard. All I remember is waking up with two bad chicks in my bed. Shit got wild that night.

"That spa treatment is exactly what I needed," I stated to my self while making my way out the spa center and on to meeting John for this boat ride and fishing trip.

"Yo, was up John how was golfing?" I questioned.

"It was dope actually, I've never been to a golf course that overlooks the beach!" he expressed with excitement.

"Oh word, that's was up," I said.

"How was your spa treatment?" he questioned, as we began leaving the pavilion and walking toward the docks.

"No lie that shit was amazing, my nigga. I was getting scrubbed down by some fine ass Spanish woman," I expressed.

"Oh word my nigga, shit I might have to check it out," he replied.

We got to the docks where the Captain polity greeted us as we stepped on board. The ship wasn't big but that bitch sure was fast. John wanted to get blazed while we gilded through the Pacific ocean. So he bought a Snoop Dogg vaporizer pen. It allows you to stuff bud in a chamber inside the pen, when you push the button on the pen it heats up the bud without smelling like weed. I use it sometimes in public when I want to get blazed. I took out my Beats Pill, turned that bitch up to the max and let Jay Z's "Big Pimpin" take over the vibe. We starting slowing down as the Captain told us that we where approaching the fishing spot. The Captain pre-baited our fishing rods so we just got straight to fishing.

"Fuck bruh, this shit is hard as fuck, slippy ass fish!" John frustratedly expressed.

"Oh don't get in your feelings now, cause you can't fish" I said while laughing.

"Shut the fuck up!" he said while finally catching something.

"Man what the fuck is this?" He angrily expressed.

"Stupid ass baby ass tuna fish, fuck this shit Dre!" he stated as we busted out laughing.

"I feel you nigga I'm hungry anyway," I said.

"Yeah me too, we've been at this shit for a few hours. Lets go grab dinner and some drinks back at the resort," he stated as he told the Captain to take us back to the docks. John and I decided to shower up and get fresh for dinner. I placed my Beats Pill outside the shower and, listened to one of my favorite joints by Wale "The God Smile."

After getting out the shower feeling ever so clean and fresh, I felt like ending the night in some comfortable attire. So I threw on an all red puma sweatsuit with some new Nike Air Force ones, ultra fly knit University Reds with the red face gold Rolex to match. Shortly, I met back up with John under the pavilion. "Dre, what the fuck!" he stated. "This isn't hood nigga fashion week in Inglewood!"

"Damn John, hop off, you know I get fresh wherever I go!" I responded with a smirk.

"Whatever young nigga, let's head over to this food spot," he stated as we made our way out the pavilion. The set up of the bar and diner was simple but dope. It was built around this big ass ceiba tree. We took our seats damn near on the outskirts of the bamboo overhang, so we could be low-key while we blazed up out of John's vape pen. A waiter came over and took our order. We decided to try there fish tacos and split a cheese pizza. We also ordered some fresh strawberry and kiwi juice. As we waited for our food, we decided now was the perfect time to get a little faded.

"Yo, so how are we rolling out tomorrow?" I questioned while passing John the vape pen.

"Set your alarm for 7:00 a.m., it's an hour drive to Granda where the cigar shop is located," he stated. "You already know I'm going to roll some blunts for us to smoke as we ride"

"Alright that's wassup" I said, as our food finally arrived. "These fish tacos and pizza is hittin' my nigga!" I expressed, as I was having a serious food-gasm.

"My nigga you ain't never lied!" he expressed while cleaning his plate. "You ready to get out of here Dre?" he tiredly questioned.

"Yeah I'm going to take the rest of this pizza to go," I replied while he called the waiter over to pay the bill.

After John paid the bill we dipped out, full as fuck and high as hell. John immediately went to his room and passed out on the bed. I knew that he was tired, but God damn I could hear this nigga snoring before I even got to my room. I got undressed, set my alarm, closed my eyes and drifted off into a deep sleep. Bone Thugs and Harmony, "Thuggish Bone" woke me up precisely at 7:00 a.m. Slowly I got out the bed while still feeling a little bit tired. I then hopped in the shower and thought about my attire for the day. Sixteen minutes later I hopped out the opened shower. I finally decided to go with a business causal feel. So I threw on my white & black Lacoste polo shirt, black H&M slacks, black Louis Vuitton belt and black Louis Vuitton loafers to match. Just to add a little sauce, I threw on my plain face sliver Rolex then proceeded out my room and into the pavilion. "

Yo wassup John, how you sleep?" I questioned.

"Like a motherfuckin' baby my nigga!" he expressed, as he rolled the last blunt for our hour journey.

"You better have my nigga, I heard your old ass snoring before I even got to my room," I stated.

"Oh word" he replied as he grabbed the keys to the Benz.

"Well fuck all that, you ready to get up outta here?" he questioned.

"Hell yea lets dip my nigga!" I replied as we left the pavilion and hopped in the Benz and sped off to Granda. Twenty minutes into our journey and I was already high fuck. I decided to get blazed to the the max, so I told John to pull the top back up so we could hot box the whip. Five blunts later and we were finally entering into the heart of Granda. We were so fucking hungry, so we drove around looking for spots to eat. Then we stumbled open this breakfast spot called "The Garden Cafe."

John parked up on the curb, and then we dipped out the car into the cafe. We approached the front counter and began to order our food. I decided to have a breakfast burrito and blueberry pancakes with some freshly squeezed orange juice. After ordering our food we sat down and patiently waited.

"Yo John, are you trying to sight see before we go into the cigar spot?" I questioned.

"Hell yeah, I like the vibe from this city; it's really colorful but at the same time chill," he expressed, as our food arrived.

"Alright we're just going to walk around for a good minute," I replied while tearing up my food.

After finishing our breakfast we walked around the cobblestone streets of Granda. Everything was so colorful and loud, but all so relaxing at the same time. We walked around several blocks until we saw this book store called Lucha Libro Books. They had all kinds of books in Spanish and we eventually bought a few. The store owner recommended us to go to this chocolate shop called Casa Chocolate. It was right around the block so we walked over and picked up a couple bars of their rich milk chocolate. While walking out of Casa Chocolate we spotted a art gallery a block over. So we decided to look at some Nicaraguan art before we headed to the cigar spot. The art at Gallery Ubago was so dope. I like the style of Nicaraguan art it's just really warm and colorful.

"Yo Dre, lets dip up outta here; I forgot I scheduled a time slot at the cigar spot," he stated.

"Damn my nigga you're slippin' but fuck it lets dip," I replied.

"No lie I am, that weed we've been smoking has a brother forgettin' " he responded as we made our way out and onto the cigar spot. "Here it is Dre, Mombacho Cigar Shop" he expressed with excitement.

The cigar shop was bigger than I expected. It was a yellow and white two level building with a lot of rooms. We were politely greeted as we walked in. John told the employe who greeted us that we were here for a two o'clock rolling session. We were then escorted into one of the rooms on the second level, where we were politely greeted by one of the master cigar rollers. He already had a bunch of raw tobacco and sheets of tobacco leaf ready for us to roll up. He then told us that we were going to be rolling three types of cigars: robusto extra, short robusto and cigarrito. Basically a long cigar, thick cigar, a short thick cigar, and a blunt size cigar. As we started rolling I quickly realized there is a big difference between rolling blunts and hand rolling cigars. First you have to align two sheets of tobacco roll your tobacco, then cut one of the ends of the cigar and put it into a presser for few minutes. From there you can wrap it in another sheet of tobacco or just smoke it as is. John and I rolled all three cigars. By the end of our session we got the hang of it. We decided to take a few sheets of tobacco to go, so we could roll up some real cigars.

"Dre we have to go to this little bar spot that I peeped around the corner earlier," John stated, as we were leaving the cigar shop.

"Alright bet, when though?" I questioned.

"I thinking later on tonight, a brother needs to shower up and change first," he stated.

"Yeah me too, alright cool say no more," I replied, as we made our way to the whip, hopped in, dropped the top, and sped off back to the resort. An hour later and we pulled back up to the resort. We immediately hopped out and headed to our rooms to shower up and get ready for the night. I headed up to my room and picked out my fit. I felt like getting stupid street fresh. So I laid out my white and gold stripped OVO tracksuit jacket and white and gold stripped sweatpants to match. Plus my very new and exclusive all white and gold OVO X Jordan 12's with a nice all gold Citizens watch just for a little sauce. After hopping out the open shower feeling so relaxed and fresh, I quickly got dressed and met John under the pavilion.

"You ready to go my nigga?" John asked.

"Hell yea, I didn't get fresh for nothing," I replied, as we left the pavilion.

We pulled back up in the beautiful, colorful city of Granda an hour later.

"Yo John park up in a good, well lit spot, I'm not trying to come back and the whip is gone," I expressed.

"I got you my nigga," he replied as he parked on the curb of the bar.

The vibe inside the bar was lit as fuck. There was mad females salsa dancing and bustin' smooth Dutty Wines all on the dance floor. John and I decided to be real low-key and observe the environment. So we posed up at the end of bar and ordered a double shot of D'usse to start off the night.

"Yo Dre peep those fine ass red bone sisters headed our way," John expressed, while downing his first shot.

"Hey, would y'all like to come dance with us," one of ladies said.

John and I looked at each other as he downed his second shot and I downed both shots. I grabbed the hand of the beautiful light-skin woman with the long thick cornrows that almost ran

33

down pass her thick hips. She looked into my eyes with a passionate stare and guided me to the middle of the dance floor where we danced to salsa and merengue music. Then the DJ threw on a reggae classic "Hold Yuh" by Gyptian. That's when shorty really started showing out. I'm talking about her ass was in motion. Her soft back side moved side to side, up and down, and honestly a brother thought he was going to bust on himself; she sure knew how to Dutty Wine. She then turned around, took my hand and lead me back to the bar.

"I like the way you move," she stated, as she ordered a glass of Bel Air champagne.

"Naw belove-it I like the way you move," I replied with a smirk.

"My name is Alicia by the way," she stated with a beautiful smile.

"Nice to be in your presence, you can just call me Dre," I replied as John and her friend met us back at the bar.

We all sat talked, laughed and got drunk as fuck. So much so, that John and I were too drunk to make the hour drive back to the resort. So Alicia and her friend told us we could stay the night at there hotel. After near stumbling into their hotel suite, from a very long night of dancing and drinking, I already knew what was about to pop off once we got up in their rooms. Alicia and I had a chemistry that was way beyond the bubbling point, especially as drunk as we were. Once John and Alicia's friend closed their room door, we closed ours. I don't kiss and tell too much but lets just say it goes down in Nicaragua.

The sunlight beamed all throughout the hotel suite as morning broke, somehow waking us all up simultaneously. Alicia and I woke up gazing into each other's eyes. She had a huge smile as she kissed me on the lips. Then she hopped out of bed to put on some sweats. My god, I'm glad she's just as beautiful when I'm sober. Man you wouldn't believe the tens I thought I brought home off a drunk night. Only to wake up in the morning and look at them like what the fuck.

We all met up in the living room of the suite. Alicia's friend gave her that *I know you just got some look.* Then Alicia gave her that, *girl I know you just got some look too.* Then they both started bustin' out laughing.

"What's so funny?" John playfully expressed.

"Oh nothing just a little inside joke," Alicia's friend replied while licking her lips at John. Then John and I looked at each other and started bustin' out laughing.

"Do y'all want to go get some breakfast?" I questioned, while looking at Alicia and her friend.

"As long as y'all niggas is buying!" Alicia's friend expressed.

"Well damn!" John expressed, with a laugh.

"John you know damn well I at least deserve some breakfast for how well I performed for you last night," Alicia's friend stated.

"Damn no lie; your right, shit you deserve to be on a nigga's honor roll the way you were showing out!" John expressed.

"O.K let's go get ready girl, we'll be right back gentlemen," Alicia stated while looking at her friend with an awkward smirk.

"Yo my nigga, how was that shit?" I curiously questioned.

"Shit no lie my nigga that shit was right I mean really, really right!" John expressed with a cheesy grin.

"Word my nigga," I replicd.

"Word up, but how was yours?" he questioned.

"I'm going to come clean, I don't really remember. I was too fucked up from last night," I stated.

"Nah nigga I believe you, your baby ass was borderline white boy wasted," he expressed as we both began to laugh.

"What's so funny?" Alicia's friend questioned. "I know y'all big headed niggas ain't in here talking shit!" Alicia's friend playfully expressed, as they were coming out of there rooms.

"And if we were, what you going to do about it punk?" John playfully replied as he walked up to her, grabbed her by the waist, and kissed her on the lips.

We all dipped out the suite and headed to this breakfast spot the girls had been eating at while they had been on there vacation. It was called "Cafe 4 Gatos." It was a really low-key breakfast spot that had outside sitting. Since it was really warm with a cool breeze every now and again, I suggested that we eat outside. A waiter saw us taking our seats and automatically came out to give us our menus. The waiter then came back a couple minutes later to take our order. The girls ordered first, then John, and finally me. I decided to have the Omega 3 Special which consisted of toast, smoke salmon, cream cheese with sliced tomatoes and capers with a fresh glass of orange juice.

After the waiter took our orders we all just started talking about how beautiful the city of Granda was. Not to much into the conversation and the waiter came back with our food. I immediately began to dive in on my plate.

"God damn Dre!" John expressed. "Even in the presence of beautiful women you still eat like the food is going to run off the plate."

"Oh I expect Dre to be a sloppy eater, especially after last night" Alicia expressed with a smirk.

"Well damn that's how your rockin' Dre?!" John questioned with a laugh.

"Well you know how it is, when your gone off that brown," I jokingly stated, and then we all busted out laughing.

John and I decided to let the girls come back to the resort since we loved their great vibes. After we all finished breakfast they went back to their hotel to grab some clothes and their bikinis. We went to go pick up the whip, thank God nobody drove off with it. Then we picked them up outside of their hotel and sped off to make our hour journey back to the resort. As we pulled up to the resort I was thinking to myself about how much I needed this. A solid hour of being caked up in the back of a nice whip, nothing but peace, relaxation and some good pussy to balance me out. John parked the whip by our suite, we all hopped out and headed into the pavilion.

"Holy shit!" Alicia's friend expressed.

"This is a nice ass suite, what line of work did y'all say y'all were in?" Alicia's friend questioned.

"Well damn nosy rosy, you ask more questions than the IRS," John jokingly replied.

"Aye look, fuck all that. I'm about to hit this warm ass shower, are you coming Alicia?" I playfully but seriously questioned.

"Sure Dre, I wouldn't mind scrubbing your dirty ass down," she playfully replied as we started walking to my room.

"YO DRE, ARE YOU STILL TRYING TO LOSE MONEY IN GOLF!" John shouted.

"FUCK YOU NIGGA, I'M GOING TO TAKE YOUR COINS. MEET ME ON THAT BITCH AT THREE O'CLOCK!" I shouted.

"ALRIGHT BET!" he shouted back.

Later, Alicia and I got undressed and hopped in the shower. This woman's body was so beautiful under the sun. Her skin had an amazing glow. The way her energy had me feeling was crazy. She didn't even mind washing me down, it's like she took pride and pleasure in nurturing a man she just met on a drunken night. After our shower we changed up and decided to go walk on the beach. We headed out the pavilion and onto the beach shore.

"So Dre if you don't mind me asking, what do you do for a living?" Alicia asked as the low tide waves crashed against our feet.

"Naw I don't mind, I'm in the marijuana industry," I stated.

"Oh so you're one of those legal drug dealers," she jokingly expressed.

"Ha-ha pretty much," I stated with a slight chuckle.

"How is that line of work?" she curiously questioned.

"It's cool — long hours, good vibes and extremely potent high quality weed," I replied.

"What made you want to get into that industry?" she curiously questioned.

"Growing up in the south side of Chicago, I didn't know any doctors or lawyers to look up to," I stated.

"Just drug dealers, pimps and stick-up kids," I expressed. "So I learned the art of hustlin' from the drug dealers on my block."

"But seeing them getting locked up, robbed and killed always turned me off from illegal hustlin', so when the laws changed I immediately seized the opportunity," I stated.

"Wow that's some wild shit," she replied with a puzzled look, as if she couldn't imagine that reality.

"I know but that was my reality. But enough of about me, what do you do for a living?" I questioned.

"My job isn't as fun or exciting as yours. I'm a day trader on Wall Street," she replied.

"What made you want to do that?" I questioned.

"Honestly I really don't know it's just something I stumbled onto, but I'm getting kind of bored with it," she stated.

"What is your passion in life?" I questioned.

"Hmm I would have to say my passion is to have kids and travel around the world," she replied. "What is your passion besides what your doing now?"

"My passion would be to get married and start a family, but I just haven't found that right woman yet," I stated.

"Why do you think that is?" she questioned.

"I would have to say my work. I spend weeks away from home bustin' my ass off and staying on my grind, so I have more wealth to retire on when the time comes" I replied as we both stopped in our tracks to admire the beautiful crystal clear waves.

"Sounds fucked up, but you're a really special spirit" she stated.

"I'm sure you'll find that right woman, who knows she could be right up under you now," she expressed as looked me in the eyes and kissed me on the lips.

"Damn Alicia!" I expressed as we pulled away from each other. She chuckled a little bit then smiled. I told her we had to go meet John and her friend on the golf course, so we left the beach and headed to the golf course.

"Oh, so look who brought their sorry ass to lose all of their coins," John stated as Alicia and I approached the golf course.

"Fuck you nigga, lets get this shit started," I stated.

"Say less," John replied as we all got in the caddy and drove to the first hole.

We pulled up to the first hole and the girls stayed in as they already expressed that golf was boring as fuck to them. So they just decided to watch us from inside the caddy. John and I hopped out and took our positions. John began to take out a driver club from the golf bag. He looked at me with a grin as he lined his club up with the ball and on the first shot he scored a hole in one.

"YEAH YOUNG NIGGA, YOU GOT ME FUCKED ALL THE WAY UP!" John shouted in excitement as the girls laughed and looked at us with one of those *nigga it's not that serious* faces. Then I shot a hole in one.

"YEA NIGGA, WHAT'S UP NOW?!" I shouted.

"Young nigga, don't get too hype, we have eight more holes to go," John stated.

On the second hole it took John and I two shots each to score. The third hole was difficult for both of us. It took me four shots and it took John three shots. On the fourth, fifth, sixth and eighth holes, we both shot a hole in one. The second to the last hole was starting to get intense. I shot a hole in one and John shot one time but got it in on the second shot. Now the last hole of the game and shit just got real. We were tied up. John was up first, he looked me in my eyes, smiled, and shot a hole in one.

"Fuck!" I said under my breath.

"Yeah, fuck is right young nigga, lets see what you do," he stated. I shot my first shot and fell short by a couple of centimeters and just like that I lost.

"FUCK, FUCK, FUCKKK!" I shouted.

"YEAH YOUNG NIGGA, RUN ME MY STACK, YOU KNOW WHAT THIS IS!" he yelled.

After my loss on the golf course we headed back to our suite. We decided to surprise the girls with dinner on the beach. We had the resort set up a barbecue with some of the fish we caught the day before.

"Wow y'all really didn't have to do this," Alicia stated as we approached the beach.

"Girl I don't know what you talking about, they better have," Alicia's friend stated.

"Shut up, old ungrateful ass," John playfully stated.

It was really all good vibes and laughter as we sat down and begin to eat. Everything was just so perfect. The sun was starting to set as the cool air rolled in. The resort hooked us up with some bottles of Bel Air champagne so we all got a little vibe off the bubbly. After John and Alicia's friend finished their meal, they went to his room. He took one of the bottles of Bel Air with him, so I already knew what type of situation he was about to have. Alicia wanted to hop in the jacuzzi, so we went to my room to change. Her body was looking so good, her hips were so thick, and her ass was so fat you could see that bitch poking out from the front. God damn I got lucky with this one. As the moonlight grew more intense, so did our vibe. Especially when we hopped in the jacuzzi with two full glasses of champagne. Alicia was super lit off the Bel Air. She started to get all up under me and whisper words that could only be carried out with physical actions.

"Alicia your cuttin' up tonight," I stated. "I think it's time we go to bed"

"I thought you would never ask," she replied as we both got out the jacuzzi and headed up to my room. "Oh look what we have here, Dre's R&B playlist. O.K, you got my favorite singer on here," she stated, as she played "I Just Want It" by Keyshia Cole.

Then she started to dance for me. At this point I knew she was definitely drunk. Then she played "I Remember" by Keyshia Cole and that's when shit go real.

"Dre!" she flirtatiously expressed, as she climbed on top of me.

As I held her by her waist she gently started to run her soft hands down my chest. Then she leaned forward and kissed me on the lips. From that point things got real X rated in Nicaragua that night.

The next morning I woke up mad early so I could catch my flight to Atlanta. Poor Alicia, she passed out before we could go for a round two. I had already packed all my luggage expect for my outfit. I felt like dressing on the business casual side. So I laid out a white & black Christian Dior polo shirt, navy H&M slacks, black sliver buckle Christian Dior belt, black Hermes loafers and a sliver tone Michael Kors watch. Then I hopped in the shower and enjoyed my last open shower in Nicaragua. Sixteen minutes later I hopped out and got dressed. I called the resort and told them to get a helicopter ready for me, since John was staying for a couple more days. I also told them to have the chef cook everyone some breakfast. The last thing I did was write Alicia a note attached with my number. I then kissed her on the forehead as she slept. And just like that I was on my way to catch a thirty minute helicopter ride to the airport.

After thirty long minutes on the helicopter I finally made it to the airport. I immediately hopped out and got my bags checked in. I then headed up to the gate of my flight to board. My late ass got there just in time. They had just started announcing my flight to board. I checked my ticket and took my first class seat by the widow of course. Then I took out some special cookies I had, ate them and waited for the effects to kick in. Shortly after I started to fade out into a deep sleep as we were taking off to Atlanta, Georgia.

CHAPTER IV

"Excuse me sir, excuse me," the stewardess said, as I began to open my eyes. "My apologies for waking you, but we've landed."

"Oh no problem, you're good," I replied as I wiped my eyes and stretched my body.

Man those weed cookies aren't no joke. If you fuck around and eat too many, your ass could be passed out for half a day. I took a few seconds to get myself together and then I grabbed my carry on luggage from the top compartment above. Finally I made my way out the plane and down the terminal. Then I took the train to baggage claim to scoop up the rest of my luggage. After picking up my luggage, I headed out of Hartsfield-Jackson Atlanta International Airport. I walked around to the car rental spot and picked up a 2015 Lexus IS C drop-top coupe. Finally I'm in ATL shawty, where it's hotter than a ten piece from the local American Deli out this bitch. I put all my luggage in the back seat and hopped in the Lexus. I dropped that mother fuckin' top back, plugged in my AUX cord and blasted my favorite song off Rick Ross's mixtape "Black Dollar" called "Money Powder" as I sped out of the airport and on to the highway.

As I was speeding up I-85 north trying not to get caught in messy ass Atlanta traffic, I was just doing some thinking about my spending habits. Maybe I should calm down on all the designer shit. I mean don't get me wrong, this shit is clean, but I think it's about that time to start saving for a family. But first I'm about to go fuck up some commons with Niniette at Phipps Plaza and Lenox mall.

Before I knew it I was exiting off the highway and onto Lenox road. Then past Peachtree and Stratford road, where my five luxurious hotel called the "Mandarin Oriental" was located. I parked the whip out front as the bellhop approached me. He politely greeted me and took all of my luggage to bring to my suite. Then valet came around and did his job. I walked into the lobby and checked into the Premier Terrace Suite, which was an apartment like suite. It had two balconies that had amazing views, one overlooking the chic boutiques of Peachtree and the other overlooking Phipps Plaza. After checking in, I made my way up the elevator and down the hall to my suite where the bellhop was waiting for me. I politely thanked him and tipped him a fifty dollar bill. Personally I like to give great tips to employees of demeaning jobs and seeing the surprise happy looks on there faces.

Soon as I stepped into the suite I immediately called Niniette. Hopefully she doesn't trip, even though I was suppose to have texted her when I landed.

"Hey Dre, wasn't you suppose to been text me?" she asked with a calm tone that surprised me.

"Niniette don't trip, I slick forgot but I'm calling now," I smoothly replied.

"Dre don't give me that smooth talking shit, like I'm one of your tricks!" she expressed. "I just wanted to make sure you were safe. I'm going to pick you up in a hour to go shopping, be ready."

"Alright I got you," I replied just before we hung up.

Before I went shopping with Niniette I texted one of my plugs in Atlanta. I told him to come through with twenty-eight grams of some great gas. He told me he would be here in forty-five minutes with my order. So to kill time I went and grabbed my chromecast flash drive from my luggage. I plugged into the flat screen and played one of my favorite podcasts on YouTube called "The Brilliant Idiots" with Charlamagne The God and Andrew Schulz. As I was dying laughing from there funny ass podcast when I heard a knock at the door. I got up, looked through the peep hole and saw that it was my plug.

"Yo what's good my nigga, you straight?" my plug questioned, as we dapped hands.

"Yeah I'm good, but now I'll be even better thanks to you," I replied as I dapped him up with the two-sixty-five.

He then handed me my order in a McDonald's bag. "Everything is here?" I questioned.

"With extra" he replied.

"That's what I'm talking about!" I happily expressed. We then dapped hands again as he dipped out.

Niniette texted me and told me she was right in front of the hotel. I put my bud up, turned off the TV and dashed out the suite, right down the hall, to the elevator, rode that down to the main lobby and then I saw Niniette's beautiful ass in her chromed out 2016 Mercedes G wagon. "Well hello there, you look mighty handsome!" Niniette expressed, as I hopped in her whip.

"You know how I do, but fuck all that, I see you in that sun dress," I stated appreciatively.

"Which one of your niggas are you showing out for?" I jokingly questioned.

"Dre don't play me, you know you're the only nigga I'm fucking," she stated. "But aye, you know how these niggas will trick on some shit they're never going to get."

"Facts," I replied in agreement as she sped off from the hotel and headed to Phipps Plaza.

Ten minutes and we were pulling up in one of the fresh paved parking spots of Phipps Plaza. "Let's go spend some hard earned bread, Dre," Niniette said as I opened the door for her for to enter the mall.

"Oh look at you being a gentleman — about time," she stated.

"Don't play me you know how I rock, I've been on gentlemen shit," I replied, as we entered into the Saks Fifth Avenue department store.

"Oh shit Dre, this is a dope ass shoulder bag!" Niniette expressed as she picked up the burgundy python skin shoulder bag.

"God damn Niniette, that shit looks real nice and real expensive" I stated.

"Nigga shut up, you stay with expensive shit. You're going to buy me this bag!" she sternly expressed.

"Whatever, hurry that-ass-up" I playfully replied, as I smacked her on her fat, soft backside.

"Damn Daddy stop!" Niniette playfully expressed with a laugh.

"Don't start with that Daddy shit," I warned. "You always say that shit as soon as I'm about to buy your fine ass something."

"Dre shut the fuck up, you already know when we get into your favorite sneaker store in Lenox you're going to have me buy you every color shell toe Adidas that you already have," she replied as I swiped my card and paid for the bag.

After we finished checking out the Celine section, we headed over to the Dior section so Niniette could look at some heels she saw online. "Yes they have them!" she expressed with excitement, as she picked up some light pink pumps.

"That's all you want?" I questioned.

"Yes Daddy," she replied with a flirtatious tone and smile as we approached the register. Then we headed to the Louis Vuitton section, where she saw a dope ass light pink Louis bag. "Daddy this bag is only four stacks can I get it?" she childishly questioned with a huge grin.

"GOD DAMN HOW MUCH?" I questioned. "You know what, fuck it, don't even tell me just get it." Then we headed to the register to check out.

"Alright Dre, lets go downstairs to the Tory Burch store and then we can hit Lenox so I can spurge on you" she said, as we headed out Saks Fifth Avenue and down the escalator to the Tory Burch store.

"Yo Niniette, I like these suede loafers, these shits are your style," I stated.

"Yeah I like these a lot," she stated, while picking up a blue suede and black suede pair. "Daddy can I get this watch too?" she childishly questioned.

"Yes shorty you know I got you," I replied as we approached the register. See that's why I love my relationship with Niniette. Whenever I'm around her it's like I can just relax and truly be myself. I love her attitude as well, she's never scared to put me in place.

"Alright Dre I'm ready, lets go head to Lenox so I can spoil you," she stated, as she pinched my cheeks and gave me a quick kiss on the lips. We headed out the first level entrance of Phipps, to the parking lot and finally we got in the whip and peeled off to Lenox.

"Niniette park closer to the entrance," I stated, as Niniette was trying to find a place to park.

"Dre I got this," she sternly stated.

"Well, excuse the Hell out of me," I jokingly replied.

"Don't get smacked up in the middle of this parking lot, Dre," she warned as she parked up by the entrance.

"Yeah nigga, you better have parked where daddy told you to," I stated under my breath as we hopped out the car.

"Nigga what?" she questioned. "Speak up pussy ass boy!"

"Shut up" I jokingly replied as I snatched her up by the waist and gave her a big kiss on the forehead and then proceeded to hold her hand as we walked into the mall.

"Dre where you want to go first?" Niniette questioned.

"Let's go to the Armani store," I replied as we took the escalator up to the third floor and continued past a couple of stores.

"Alright Dre, get what your going to get," she stated as we entered into Armani Exchange. "Yo Dre, how do you like this navy & white zip up hooded jacket?" she questioned, as she brought the jacket to me.

"This shit is dope, it would go perfect with my navy and white mid top Air Forces. I don't see anything else I want, so we can check out and head up to the Ralph Lauren store," I stated, as we made our way to the register.

After we finished up at the register, we took the escalator up to the fourth level and then headed into the Ralph Lauren store. Immediately I saw some dope ass, big polo shirts. I snatched up about three shirts as Niniette came up to me with two fly ass button-downs. "I know you like these button-downs" she stated with a smile.

"Hell yeah, them shits are clean as Hell," I replied as we approached the register. Then after we finished up at the register, we headed down past Neiman Marcus and into the Zara store. "Alright Dre, just stay posed up by the fitting room and I'm going to pick out a few slacks for you," she said.

"Say less," I replied as I headed over to the fitting rooms.

She came back over with three pairs of slacks: a navy, tan and linen pair. "Try these on Dre" she said. These shits fit nice, I thought to myself after trying on the last pair. "Yea lets go ahead and get all three," I said to Niniette, as I came out the fitting room.

45

"Alright let's go check," she stated as we headed to the register. "Alright Dre, lets make the next store the last one."

"Well damn, I don't remember rushing you," I replied with one of those *you got me fucked up* type of looks.

"Nigga shut up and fix yo' god damn face!" she expressed. "I made reservations for dinner, and you know I don't play that late shit like some people I know."

"Oh so you sneak dissin' now," I playfully replied, as we made our way past the Apple store and into the Adidas store. I didn't take too much time in the Adidas store since I already knew what I wanted. I just snatched up a pair of all-white shell toes and then we bounced.

"Yo lets go to the Godiva store, I want to scoop up some chocolate bars," I stated as we left the Adidas store.

"Nigga, what the fuck did I just say," she sternly replied.

"Aye, keep your mother fuckin' voice down before I bat you in your shit," I jokingly whispered in her ear.

"Dre!" she expressed with a chuckle and a grin. "Don't play, you know I'll put hands on you boy."

"Lets go to to god damn chocolate store," she stated, as we walked down past the Abercrombie & Fitch store and headed into to the Godiva store. "Oh shit I didn't know they had these!" Niniette said, as she picked up a box of dark chocolate dipped strawberries. I then picked up a couple of milk chocolate bars as we proceeded to check out.

After we finished up at the Godiva store we took the elevator down to the first level and then headed out the entrance and to the whip.

"HURRY UP PUTTIN'-EM BAGS IN THE TRUNK!" Niniette shouted, as she started up the car.

"AYE WHAT DID I TELL YOU ABOUT RUSHING ME!" I shouted back.

"NIGGA SHUT YO PUNK ASS UP, BEFORE I LEAVE OUT THIS BITCH!" she shouted back.

"Fuck you," I playfully stated as I hopped in the passenger side.

"THIS IS MY SHIT DRE!" Niniette shouted as she turned up "Are You That Somebody" by late great Aaliyah.

"Yo fuck all that, are we almost there yet a nigga is hungry as fuck," I impatiently stated.

"Nigga don't give me that shit, when I was trying to get your goofy ass up outta Lenox so we could eat," she stated.

"Damn, you're right," I replied with a sigh.

"Nigga I know I am, but we're almost here, it's just right around the corner," she said. "See nigga, I told you it was right around the corner" she stated, as we pulled to the low key restaurant called "Southern Art."

After Niniette parked, we hopped out the car and made our way inside. "Jackson, party for two," Niniette said, after we were politely greeted.

"O.K, right this way," the waitress said as she guided us to our table. She then told us another waiter will be over shortly to take our order. Not even a split second later and a waiter comes rushing over and handing us menus.

"Oh no thank you, we won't be needing menus we already know what we want," Niniette stated. "We will be having the Buttermilk Fried Chicken and the Cajun Jambalaya Pasta."

"O.K what would you like to drink?" the waiter questioned.

"We'll have a glass of Chateau Baulac Dodijos Sauternes from your dessert wine collection and also a glass of water," she replied.

"O.K I'll be right back with your drinks," the waiter said.

"So when did you start ordering my food" I stated.

"Dre shut up and trust me, you're going to like it, but anyway what's new with you?" she questioned.

"Nothing much," I replied. "Wait, oh shit I forgot to tell you about this girl I met the day we had lunch at IL Foranio's," I told her.

"What's good with her, is she cute?" she questioned as the waiter brought our drinks and told us our food will be ready shortly.

"Nigga do you even have to ask, you know how I play," I replied.

"Well Mr. Player I hope you're wrappin' up," she stated with a chuckle.

"Nah it's not even like that," I replied.

47

"Wait hold up, so y'all haven't fucked?" she questioned with a surprise look on her face.

"Nah that next day I invited her over, cooked for her, and the whole nine," I said. "Then I fell asleep after getting faded and I woke up the next morning and shorty was gone," I said.

"OH SHIT, HOMEGIRL WORKED THAT ASS!" she loudly said while bustin' out into laughter.

"Aye believe that shit if you want, but I got something planned real nice for shorty as soon as I touch back down," I stated as the waiter came back with our food.

"I told you this shit is good as fuck," she said, as I was tearing up my chicken.

"Shit, you ain't never lied," I replied.

Twelve minutes later and we had already finished our plates clean. Niniette called the waiter over and asked for the check. Then a minute later she paid the bill and tipped the waiter a fifty.

"Aww look at you being generous," I stated.

"Nigga shut up, I'm always generous but fuck all that, lets get up out of here," she said as we both got up and made our way out the door onto the parking lot. Then we hopped in the whip and sped off back to my hotel. "Alright Dre, I'm going to call you first thing in the morning tomorrow to make sure you're up," Niniette stated as she pulled up to the hotel.

"Alright cool," I said as she popped the trunk so I could get my bags.

"ALRIGHT DRE, SEE YOU TOMORROW!" she shouted as I was walking into the hotel.

I entered into the lobby and headed for the elevator. I rode the elevator up to my level, hopped out and made way down the hall to my suite. As soon as I opened the door and walked in, I immediately dropped my bags and ran to the bathroom. A brother had to piss. After, I took my chromecast flash drive out of the living T.V and hooked it up took the bedroom T.V. I wanted to get high as hell and watch one of my favorite hood movies "Menace II Society." I hopped in the comfortable king sized bed with my twenty eight grams and started to roll a few fat ass joints.

As I got more into the movie, while the effects from the good bud I had started to kick in, I realized this movie really meant something to me. Since a youngin' I was surrounded by the harsh realities of growing up in the hood. I mean I am from a city nicknamed Chiraq. "Menace II Society" may be a crazy ass movie for some, but for me it was my reality. Thank god I had the knowledge of business so I didn't fall into the trap of gang bangin' and illegal drug slangin'. But at the same time I was inspired by the dealers on my block too.

Honestly the only thing that separated me from a corner hustler is knowledge. All I wish is that my brothers on the south side of Chicago could come together and start a petition to legalize weed. All they would have to do is present an initiative to state congress and then start a campaign to make sure it gets voted on. But the reality is they won't because there to blinded by avenging the death of their fellow gang members. Which is also the part of the trap that keep blacks ignorant and divided by simple shit. So they may never come together, and come up with a plan to shift control and power into the hood, for the hood, and by the people of the hood.

God damn it's morning already, I thought to myself as my phone started to ring, sending Rick Ross's "Diced Pincapples" jamming all through my suite. "GOOD MORNING DRE!" Niniette shouted before I could even say hello.

"Morning," I said with a sleepy voice.

"Nigga you better not go back to sleep!" she sternly stated.

"Nah, I actually have a massage appointment in thirty minutes, so I'm glad you woke me up," I replied with a yawn.

"O.K cool, I'm going to pick you up at twelve, just look out for my text," she said.

"Alright cool," I said right before we hung up. I hopped out of bed and shuffled through my luggage to lay out my outfit for the day. I felt like chillin', but I wanted to wear some special fabric at the same time. So I took out my Ralph Lauren Purple Label track suit, sliver Versace watch and my all-white shell toe adidas that Niniette bought me at the mall. I also took out my Beats Pill and started to blast my favorite album by Wale: "The Album About Nothing." Then I finally hopped in the large walk-in shower.

Twenty minutes later I hopped out the shower and got dressed. I then headed out the suite, took the elevator all the way to the spa treatment floor and then checked in at the desk. The

49

beautiful dark-skin sister at the desk guided me to my spa suite. She told me to dress down to my boxers and that the masseuse would be out shortly. The masseuse came out with a rolling cart of heated stones since I was getting an aroma stone massage. It's a type of massage that generates energy for the body as well as creating a sense of balance and calmness. *God damn I knew these rocks were going to be heated but these bitches are hot,* I thought to myself as my masseuse got really into the massage.

An hour later and I woke up to the masseuse telling me I could get dressed. Man that massage definitely worked, I thought to myself as I started to get up and get dressed. I was mad hungry after my massage so I decided to get some breakfast. I exited out the spa suite then out the spa treatment level. Finally I hopped on the elevator, rode it out to the lobby, and headed outside. After the valet came and brought the whip around, I then hopped in, dropped the top, plugged in my aux cord and blasted "Juicy" by The Notorious BIG. And finally I sped off through the streets.

A few minutes later and I pulled up to Flying Biscuit Cafe. I hopped out the whip and proceeded inside. I was politely greeted upon approaching the register. I proceeded to order their Hollywood Omelette & Heavenly French Toast, which consisted of egg whites, spinach, mushrooms topped with white cheddar and warm tomato coulis and basil with a side of French toast topped with raspberry sauce & honey creme. A couple minutes after ordering and my food was already done.

I exited out the spot, made my way to the whip and hopped in then sped off back to the hotel. A couple minutes later and I parked in front of the hotel and I hopped out so the valet could do his job. I headed into the hotel, made my way to the elevator, hopped on that joint and rode it up to my level. I then hopped out and made my way down the hall and into my suite. Finally I had the chance to eat out on the balcony, which had dope ass views of the many boutiques on Peachtree. Man I love my life, I said to myself as I took a long hit of my joint. I then began to eat my breakfast while admiring the dope views from the balcony. As I was finishing up my breakfast I got a text from Niniette saying she was out front. So I took the last few bites from my meal and puffs from my joint, before heading out the suite. I made way down the hall, hopped on the elevator and rode it down to the lobby and proceeded out the hotel.

"Don't you look handsome today!" Niniette expressed with a smile as I approached her car.

"You already know, I always come clean," I replied as I hopped in the whip and she proceeded to pull off.

"Where exactly are these houses at?" I questioned as she hopped on the freeway.

"They're on the east side of Atlanta in the black suburbs of Lithonia" she said. "It's a thirty minute drive, so just sit tight and try not to get on my nerves."

"Well damn, you won't have to worry about me anyway," I said. "I smoked some good bud before you came to pick me up so I'll be asleep soon" Then before I knew it I actually started to doze off.

"Wake up nigga!" Niniette said as we finally pulled up to a huge ass neighborhood. We parked near the curb of one of the houses that me and Niniette were suppose to be buying.

"O.K Dre, all of these four houses are exactly the same as far as the interior is considered," she explained. "So we only have to look at one, is that cool with you?"

"Yeah it's cool," I replied with a yawn.

We then hopped out and proceeded to go inside of the house. The house was beautiful and spacious. It was a four bedroom, two bathroom that even had a finished basement plus movie theater space. I was already sold, but we walked around and checked all the rooms. Finally we decided to go ahead to the leasing office and do the paperwork. We walked around to the leasing office, headed in and met with a sales rep. She drew up the paperwork and checked our excellent credit. Then, before you knew it, we successfully purchased four homes.

"Alright Dre, lets go back to my spot to celebrate," she stated with a smile, as we left the leasing office and headed to the car. I didn't speak on it but already knew what she meant by celebrate. I wasn't trippin', shit I haven't had some good-good since I left Nicaragua I thought to myself as we hopped in the car and pulled off back to Niniette's apartment in Buckhead.

Thirty minutes later and we pulled up to Niniette's Buckhead apartment complex. We hopped out the whip and made

51

our way up stairs, down the hall and finally into her apartment. Since she only brought me back to fuck, I decided to mess with her.

"Dre lets go to my room," she flirtatiously stated with a smile.

"Nah I'm tired," I replied with a yawn, as I kicked my sneaks off and stretched out on the couch.

"Dre don't mother fuckin' play with me!" she sternly expressed.

"Who are you talkin' to?" I questioned. "You are buggin'"

"I'M BUGGIN', NIGGA WHO THE FUCK ARE YOU TALKIN' TO?" she angrily shouted as she stood over me pointing her fingers in my face.

"BITCH IF YOU DON'T CALM YOUR GOOFY ASS DOWN" I shouted back at her in frustration. Before I could even apologize for calling her a bitch, she popped my ass with a front hand and back hand. That shit sounded like WHOP-WHOP.

"PUSSY ASS BOY DON'T YOU EVER ADDRESS ME AS A BITCH IN YOUR LIFE" she angrily shouted as she grabbed her purse and keys, slamming the door on her way out. *Damn that went real left really fast,* I thought to myself. But I already knew how I had to make up for it.

I then went in her liquor cabinet and poured me a double of Apple Ciroc, to numb the pain of her hand going across my face. After downing both shots, I went in her fridge and grabbed some diced pineapples and mangos as well as some whole strawberries. I then proceeded to her bathroom and started to run the water until it was nice and warm. Then I went back to the kitchen to cut up the strawberries. After the tub was halfway full I got all the fruit and dumped most of it in the warm water. Then I turned off the lights in the bathroom, took a couple of scented candles from her living room and lit them. I began to hear the front door open as I was coming out her room.

"Dre" she said with clam tone.

I walked over to her and gave her a kiss on the lips as I started to undress her. After I dressed her down, I scooped her up and walked her over to the bathroom. Then I placed her in the warm tub of fruits. I connected my phone to her Beats Pill and started to play "Cater To You" by Destiny Child.

"Close your eyes" I said as I started to feed her strawberries, mangos and then her favorite: pineapples. I decided that it was time for me to go ahead and beat her back out, so I told her to get out the tub and I proceeded to oil her down.

Niniette's body was to perfect. Her thighs were nice and thick and her booty was soft as dryer sheets. Everything on this woman was amazing. Then I smacked her on her soft, fat backside and told her to get in bed and wait for daddy. I grabbed her Beats Pill and sat it on her dresser. Then I started to blast Tyrese's album "Black Rose." I hopped in bed and proceeded to drop that lumber.

I woke up a couple of hours later and grabbed my phone, seeing that it was nine-thirty. "Damn I have to go, my flight is at one tomorrow," I said to myself. I rolled over and saw that Niniette was still sleep. So I went to my Uber app and requested an Uber. I got dressed and headed outside to wait. My Uber pulled up a couple of minutes later. I hopped in and told him to stop at the nearest American Deli.

Then a couple of turns later and we were pulling up to the American Deli. I hopped out Uber then headed inside of the American Deli. I walked up to the cashier, politely greeted him, and began to order a 20 piece, extra wet, half hot, half lemon pepper and a 10 piece hot — both with lemonades. A few minutes later my order was ready, so I scooped up my food and hopped back in the Uber and headed to the hotel. Exactly twelve minutes later we pulled up to the hotel. I got my 20 piece and lemonade and hopped out the Uber.

"Wait, you're forgetting your other bag," the Uber man said.

"Nah that's for you" I said, as I walked off. I love showing random acts of kindness, it just warms my heart. I then made my way into the hotel and headed for elevator. I rode the elevator up to my level, hopped out made my way down the hall then into my suite. I sat my wings on coffee table in the living room and went to get my chromecast flash drive from the T.V and stick it in the T.V in the living room. I then played my favorite web series "Money & Violence" off my YouTube app, while I started to roll some fat ass joints. After about a good episode I had already finished my wings and joints. So I turned off the T.V, set my alarm for 10:00 a.m. and just passed out in the couch.

I woke up to Kevin Gates' song "Pride" bumping all throughout the suite. I hopped up off the couch and started packing the clothes Niniette bought me. Then I started up the shower and hopped in that bitch for a good fifteen minutes. I then stepped out the shower, rolled a few joints and laid out my fit for the day. I wanted to dress real comfortable so laid out my navy Puma sweatsuit. Then ran a warm soapy bath. I sat my Beats Pill on the marble counter top and played Kayne's album, "The Life Of Pablo." Then I slid into the warm soapy tub and proceeded to light my first joint, as I enjoyed the view of hotels garden. Forty minutes later I hopped out the tub, got dressed, put up my Beats Pill, and grabbed my luggage. I put on my all-white shell toes Adidas, hopped out the suite and down the hall, then onto the elevator and rode it down to the lobby. I checked in my room key and headed outside as the valet came around with the whip. I threw my luggage in the trunk, hopped in, dropped the top and sped off to the airport.

Twenty minutes later and I pulled into the rental section of Hartsfield-Jackson Atlanta International Airport. I checked the whip into the rental section of the airport. Then I headed into airport and checked my luggage through the first class section. I then made my way to the train and rode that down to the terminal. I hopped up on the escalator and made my way to my gate, where I waited for my flight to be called. Oh shit, I said to myself as I found a THC pill in my pocket and popped it just as my flight was being called. I bordered the flight and took my first class seat. Then I kicked back until the plane took off and landed in Seattle. A few hours later and I was waking up to the beautiful voice of the flight attendant telling me we just landed in Seattle. I got up, stretched my body, grabbed my carry on luggage and made my way off of the plane. I then headed down the terminal, all the way to baggage claim where I scooped up the rest of my luggage. Then I headed outside of the airport to the car drop off spot. I popped the trunk, threw my luggage in, hopped in and sped off to my crib.

While driving out the airport I hit up one of my old friends. He managed this little jazz spot in downtown Seattle. I just asked him for a little favor, then I called Christine to see what she was up to. "Yo Christine, was up?" I questioned, as she picked up the phone.

"Nothing much" she replied. "I haven't seen you in some weeks, is everything O.K?"

"Yeah everything is good, I had to handle some business out of town," I said. "What do you got going on tonight?"

"Nothing major just a little studying, but why wassup?" she questioned.

"Do you want to go out tonight?" I questioned.

"Sure!" she expressed with excitement.

"O.K cool, I'll pick you up later on tonight and dress to impress," I said.

"Alright Dre, I'll see you later," she replied before we hung up.

A few minutes after getting off the phone with Christine, I was pulling into my garage. I popped the trunk, hopped out and got all my luggage. I then headed into the living room then upstairs to my room. I just tossed my luggage on the floor of my walk-in closet and I set an alarm for seven o'clock as I climbed into my soft bed and passed out. A few hours later and my alarm was going off, sending Kendrick Lamar's song "Money Trees" blasting all throughout my room. I hopped out of bed and went to my walk-in closet. I grabbed my black big horse Ralph Lauren Purple Label polo shirt, black valet loafers and my black Zara slacks. Then I took my Beats Pill out my luggage and sat it up on my countertop in my bathroom. I then blasted "Track Number 2" from Kendrick Lamar's album "Untitled Unmastered" right before I hopped in the shower. Fifteen minutes later and I hopped out of the shower and got dressed. I then went into my walk-in closet and grabbed half a gram of some good Kali Mist wax, along with my Snoop Dogg vape pen. Then I headed downstairs, past the living room, out to the garage and hopped in my car to go pick up Christine from her dorm. Fourteen minutes later and I was pulling into the parking lot of Christine's dorm.

"HURRY UP!" I playfully shouted as I saw her beautiful ass coming out her dorm.

"Don't you look beautiful," I flirtatiously stated as she hopped in the passenger side.

"Well thank you, you look well groomed as usual," she replied with a shy smile.

I then pulled out the parking lot and sped off to the Jazz spot. "Where are you taking me tonight Dre?" she questioned.

"It's a surprise," I replied, as we turned into the parking of Dimitriou's Jazz Alley. "Oh shit Dimitriou's Jazz Alley!" she stated. "I wanted to kick it here and listen to some jazz for a minute now," she stated with excitement as we hopped out the whip and headed inside.

"We're going to get a table on the second level balcony are you cool with that?" I questioned.

"Yeah, I'm just glad to be here," she replied.

"As long as your rockin with me, memories like this will be your reality," I said as we made our way up to the balcony level.

We then took our seats at our table and a waiter shortly came over and took our order. I ordered us an Herb Roasted Half Chicken. It consisted of an mushroom marsala demi glaze, whipped potatoes, and seasonal vegetables. After the waiter left I took out my wax, stuffed it in my vape pen and took a long hard hit. I then told Christine I have to use the restroom. Little did she know I pulled in a couple of favors so I could hop on stage and recite a poem I wrote for her.

"Ladies & Gentlemen we have a very special performance for you tonight! Introducing my long time friend, DRE!" the announcer said, as I came from behind the curtains.

"Wassup y'all, this is your main man Dre and I will be reciting an original poem for someone very special to me," I said high as hell. Then I began to recite my poem:

The Anatomy of Love

I cleanse our ambience with the most scented of candles.

Never know how our souls will enter twine but I'm sure I can handle.

It's like when red mixes with blue and everything gets so violet,

No words spoken, only gestures in motion pure silence

To what's between your thighs. I'm heavily devoted,

Praying while I'm pressing lips against your universe.

A woman's womb creates life so can I drink the milk from your God box.

They say the body is the temple, therefore purify my body in the squirts of your holy water.

I think this is the power of God I can feel our love getting stronger.

An orgasm, climax or cum is only a God connection in sexual form

As the peak ends and turns our bodies numb;

Eye to eye, man to woman or King to God, I now know the anatomy of love.

The audience sure loved my poem. Real niggas were crying and the ladies were going crazy. I then headed back up to the balcony level. I knew Christine was up there surprised as hell.

"Did you like my poem?" I questioned.

"Dre that was beautiful!" she replied with tears in her eyes.

"Ha-ha don't cry over this good chicken," I stated with a chuckle as I wiped her eyes.

After finishing our meal and a couple glasses of red wine we decided to head back to my crib. So we made our way down the stairs, out the door and finally out to the parking lot. We then hopped in my whip and sped off back to my spot.

"Dre I had a great time tonight," she stated, as I pulled into my garage.

"I was hoping you did," I replied. "I had to pull a few favors for that performance."

"I'm pretty sure you did, Mr. Money Man," she replied with a smirk as we hopped out the whip, into the living room and up the stairs to my bedroom.

"Dre" she flirtatiously said, as she started to take her dress off.

"Wassup baby girl?" I questioned, as I got undressed and jumped on my soft California, king size bed.

"I want to read to you again Daddy," she stated, as she went to my bookshelf.

"Alright cool, grab that book on the top left and come get yo big booty ass in this bed," I stated with a grin as I grabbed a little joint from my dresser and lit it.

"'Ja Rule Tales Of An Unruly Man?'" she questioned.

"Yup that one," I said as she hopped in my bed. She then laid her head on my chest and started to read to me. Then as she got past the first chapter, she stopped reading and looked up at me. She grabbed my face and began to kiss me ever so passionately and gracefully. And after that, you already know we got to knockin' boots the whole night.

CHAPTER V

I woke up at daybreak the next morning, to a note from Christine. She expressed in the note that she had a big test in the morning so she couldn't spend the whole. I wasn't trippin' about it, I got me some cutty last night. As I was reaching in my drawer to grab a pre-rolled blunt of some good Sour OG. I noticed a glass of freshly squeezed orange juice with a strawberry wedge. See what good dick makes a woman do. *Freshly squeezed mother fuckin' orange juice,* I thought to myself as I started laughing. I took my blunt and orange juiced then walked over to my bookshelf. I picked up Damond John's "The Power Of Broke" and then proceeded downstairs and out to my terrace. I decided to read a couple of chapters before I cooked some breakfast. As I got deep into the first chapter, I realized everything in life is a hustle.

If I want to reach my billionaire goal then I need to be hustlin', as if I'm still stuck in the south side of Chicago again. I'm starting to get way too comfortable with the few million I have. I need to make some more power moves so I can not only put myself in a better position, but also upgrade my day one niggas' positions too. Damn this is some good bud, got a nigga making all types of life changing decisions and shit.

What do I feel like eating, I thought to myself as I entered in my chef's kitchen. You know what I'm just going to keep it simple, I said to myself as I took two fillets of smoked salmon out my fridge. I turned on my flat screen in the kitchen and then went to my YouTube app and played DJ Khaled interview with Hot 97. "Man, that nigga DJ Khaled is a fuckin' fool," I said while laughing to myself. But on the real he is always on point with the game he gives. I then threw both the fillets on the skillet to cook-up for a bit. God damn my salmon is looking fine I said to my self as I turned off my stove and plated my smoke salmon. I had to head out to my warehouse today, so I didn't kick back in the living room and dine like I usually would. I just ate in the kitchen while watching this funny ass nigga DJ Khaled giving these niggas the keys to success.

After I finished my breakfast I headed upstairs to my room to get undressed and hop in the shower. Before I hopped in the shower I headed over to my walk-in closet and laid out my fit. Since I wasn't doing anything major, there was no reason for me to get all the way swagged up. So I just laid out a navy and white Armani jacket, black Zara jeans and my white and navy shell toe Adidas, and I hopped in the shower. Hopefully those Jamaican plants I snatched up a couple months ago were almost done growing.I then finished up my shower and got dressed.

After getting dressed, I headed downstairs and past the living room then into the garage. I hopped in the whip, pulled out of the garage and sped off to my warehouse. Twenty minutes later I was pulling up to my warehouse. I was stupid excited to see how my Jamaican plants were turning out. I hopped out the car and made way inside.

"Dre, what's good my nigga?" my top grower questioned.

"Shit nothin' major, I just got back in town from my trip to Nicaragua and Atlanta," I replied.

"Damn nigga you stay out the country, I know you passport is stamped the fuck up," he said.

"Hell yea, you know how I move," I stated.

"You know I got some good news for you," he said.

"Oh word, what's good?" I questioned with excitement.

"That Jamaican shit as grown twice the size we thought it would," he stated.

"So that couple million you thought you were going to make, is going to be more like four to five million flat," he stated. "And if we break it down to wax, you could make twice that."

"GOD DAMN!" I loudly expressed.

"Hell yeah, my nigga" he said.

"BOOM!" door kicked in.

"EVERYBODY GET THE FUCK ON THE GROUND, FBI!" FBI agent said.

"What the fuck," I said to myself as my top grower jumped on the ground.

"EVERYBODY GET THE FUCK ON THE GROUND THIS IS A MOTHER FUCKIN' RAID!" an FBI agent angrily said, as he approached me and slammed me to be the ground.

"GOD DAMN, YOU DIDN'T HAVE TO DO ALL THAT!" I angrily shouted, as I started to see blood dripping out of my mouth.

"SHUT THE FUCK UP BEFORE I BLOW YOUR MOTHER FUCKIN' BRAINS OUT!" the FBI agent shouted back at me. Then hell of agents were just rushing to each section of my warehouse, taking my product and fucking shit up. One by one agents were taking my clones, flowers and extracts. By the time they were done I knew I would would of been a few million in the hole.

"ASK HIM WHERE HE KEEPS THE CASH!" one of the agents said to the agent that still had his foot in my ass.

"WHERE THE FUCK IS THE MONEY?" the agent questioned, as he smacked me in the back of my head.

"BITCH FUCK YOU, GO FIND IT!" I angrily shouted.

Luckily I knew better then to keep everything in one spot. You always keep your work and paper in separate spots, that's the main rule of hustlin' whether its legal or illegal.

"I'M NOT GOING TO ASK YOU AGAIN, WHERE THE FUCK IS THE MONEY?" the agent angrily questioned as he clocked his gun back.

"YOU THINK THATS SUPPOSE TO SCARE SOMEBODY?" I angrily shouted.

"IF YOUR GOING TO PULL THE TRIGGER DO IT, F-B-I AGENT!" I angrily shouted back in a mocking fashion. See if I was going to go out then I was going to go out like Pac in 1993 when he was bustin' at cops.

"FUCK YOU NIGGER!" he angrily shouted as he kicked me in the ribs.

"COME ON MAN!" another agent shouted.

Then just as they came they left. Ain't this about a bitch? I just got legally robbed. That is the problem with this legal weed shit. Federally, it's still illegal so really the Feds can come and ransack grow ops or dispensaries whenever the fuck they want to. I'm not really trippin' though, it's what I signed up for; this is what comes with the game. I'm just going to have to take this L and keep it pushin'. Shit when things get bad I just grind about it.

"IS EVERYONE ALRIGHT?" I shouted to all my workers.

"Yeah, everyone looks alright, Dre" my top grower said.

"Alright cool, get everyone together and give me a list of everything that was snatched up and everything that's tore up," I stated.

"Alright bet," my top grower said.

"And bring it to me, I'll be outside in the car. I need to make a couple of calls," I said. Then I headed outside hopped in my whip and immediately called Niniette.

"Yo wassup Dre, how are you?" Niniette said.

"To tell you the truth, I'm fucked up right now" I said with a sigh.

"How are you fucked up?" she curiously questioned.

"I just got raided a few minutes ago" I said.

"WHAT THE FUCK YOU MEAN YOU GOT RAIDED?" she yelled in the phone.

"Man the shit was crazy," I replied. "I was checking up at the warehouse and as I was just about to leave FBI kicked in the door and told everybody to get the fuck down."

"Fuck Dre, are you alright" she said with a worried tone in her voice.

"Besides one of the agents roughing me up a little bit, I'm good," I said.

"I'm still in Atlanta but I'm about to book a flight out now," she said.

"Nah chill, you don't have to do all that," I sincerely said.

"NIGGA FUCK ALL THAT, I'll BE THERE IN A FEW HOURS!" she yelled into the phone and then hung up. See that's why I love Niniette she is a real ride or die, down ass chick.

I then lit up a blunt I had in my glove box as I waited for my top grower to come back with the info. "Yo so what are we looking like?" I questioned to my top grower before he could even reach the car door.

"I'm not going to lie to you Dre, we're looking too fucked up," he stated. "Everything is gone expect for a couple of clones and wax."

"FUCK!" I angrily shouted with a sigh. "What about the Jamaican shit, do we have any left?"

"Nah Dre, all we have is a couple of clones of it" he said.

"Alright tell all the guys to put all the broken or fucked shit in a trash pile," I stated. "Anything that isn't fucked up, put it to the side for now," I said.

"Alright Dre, I got you," my top grower said before I sped off.

I was so fuckin' pissed about the raid that I didn't want to rush home, I just drove around the downtown area for some hours. Since all my Jamaican shit was gone, there was only one person I knew for sure that could hit me with some grade A work.

"Yo Ace, wassup my nigga?" I questioned as he picked up the phone.

"Shit nothin' major my nigga, just getting to this paper," he stated.

"How did that Jamaican shit move?" he questioned.

"The bud moved fast as fuck," I replied.

"Shit, that's what's up," he stated. "What about the plants though?"

"That's what I'm actually calling you about, my nigga," I said.

"What you mean, is everything straight bruh?" he questioned with a concerned tone.

"My nigga I just got raided," I said with a sigh.

"RAIDED, WHAT THE FUCK, BRUH?" he shouted.

"My nigga I know, shit is all bad right now," I said.

"What all did they take?" he questioned.

"Damn near everything but some clones and sheets of wax," I said.

"Damn my nigga even that Jamaican shit?" he questioned.

"Hell yeah, I only have a few clones of that but that's about it, my nigga," I said.

"Well looks like you hit me up just in time," he said. "I'm about to go see my connects out of Costa Rica and Columbia in two weeks. They always have official shit that's way better than that Jamaican shit anyway" he said.

"Shit alright my nigga text me the details when you get them," I replied. "We're definitely going to make that happen, I need to come ten times harder out here."

"See that's why I fucks with you, even though you just got busted, you're not letting that affect your grind," he said in a serious tone.

"You already know I can't sit up here and cry about it like no bitch," I said. "Everybody takes L's, but what determines how much of a man you are — by how you come back from a L."

"Shit nigga you ain't never lied," he replied.

"I'll hit you up with that info later, stay safe my nigga," he said.

"Alright you to," I said as we both hung up.

Damn I need to call this nigga John, I thought to myself as I was still cruisin' around downtown, bumpin' TI's album "Trap Muzik."

"Yo, my nigga," I said immediately as John answered the the phone.

"Damn Dre, you sound like your in a rush or some shit, is everything good?" he questioned.

"Nah my nigga, shit is all bad," I said.

"What's good?" he questioned.

"My nigga I just got raided," I said.

"Damn, we need to have a sit down about this, your phone could be tapped" he said.

"Yeah your right my nigga," I said in agreement.

"Alright I'm going to scoop you up tomorrow and we're going to head over to the gun range," he said. "I know that should help you blow off some steam."

"Yeah you're right my nigga, that sounds like some shit I could fuck with right now," I said.

"Facts, but keep your head up my nigga, I got some business to discuss with you anyway" he said.

"Oh word, I know your business always come with a good vacation plus a great pay day," I said.

"You already know, and vice versa" he replied. "I got some shit that's going to have you back on your feet in no time."

"Oh word? That's why I fucks with you John, you always come through even when it's crunch time" I said.

"You already know how we play, my nigga," he said.

"Hell yeah you know I know, but I'll catch you tomorrow, my nigga Niniette is calling me," I said.

"Alright my nigga, I'll hit your line," he said before we hung up.

"DRE HURRY YOUR BLACK ASS HOME, I'M COOKING!" she shouted. Before I could even ask her how she get here so fast she had already hung up, so I just made a U-turn and headed back to my crib.

"DRE!" Niniette said, as she jumped in my arms as I was walking into my living room.

"God damn, Niniette" I said with a grin.

"Shut up nigga, I'm just glad your O.K," she said, as she got off me.

"O.K Dre, just chill in the living room and relax," she stated. "I'll be in the kitchen cooking you something to eat. And I rolled up some blunts for you, plus I got a movie playing for you." Then she grabbed my face and passionately kissed me on the lips. She then headed back in the kitchen to finish cooking. She put on one of my favorite movies "The Player's Club." I sunk into my fine leather couch and proceeded to light one of the fat blunts Niniette rolled up for me. Even though I had a fucked up day, I'm still blessed to have strong people in my circle that I know I can count on when shit gets rough. But that's this thing call life, you never know what is going to happen. Sometimes you just have to just roll with the punches.

"Alright Dre, dinner is ready," Niniette stated. She brought both of our plates out and went back in the kitchen to grab a bottle of red wine.

"God damn Niniette, this buffalo grilled shrimp linguine is the shit!" I expressed. "You must of put your whole foot in it."

She came back with two wine glasses and a bottle of red wine. "You already know how I get down in the kitchen," she stated.

We both ended up enjoying our food, fine wine and a funny ass classic movie. See that's why I love having Niniette around, she can really make a brother's day. Man this woman is really special.

"Alright Dre, go head upstairs while I take care of the dishes," she said. "I have a surprise for you." She winked as she took our plates and glasses.

I already knew what she had planned for me and with the kind of day I had, I needed me some good-good. I headed up stairs and into my room, patiently waiting for her to get done with the dishes.

"Good you're already in position" Niniette stated, as she climbed on my back and started to massage my back and neck. She then connected her phone to my Beats Pill and blasted Tyrese album "Black Rose." She turned me over and started rubbing my chest. "Don't worry Daddy I got you, your in good hands," she seductively said. Then I grabbed her waist, as she began to lean in and start kissing me on the lips.

The next morning I was awaken out my sleep to the smell of something amazing. I grabbed my boxers, that somehow ended up on the other side of the room. God damn I know we got wild last night but shit, I guess the turn up was realer then I thought. I then put on my boxers and headed downstairs.

"What you over here cooking?" I questioned as I entered the kitchen.

"Your favorite: strawberry cinnamon-bun waffles with a tropical fruit smoothie," she said with a smile.

"You're the best," I said. I then grabbed her by the waist and kissed her on the lips.

"Your breakfast will be ready in a few minutes," she said. "Go blaze up out on the terrace I already rolled up a joint for you."

"Alright thanks," I said. Then I made my way out to my terrace. As I sat down and sparked up my joint, my phone began to ring. Judging by the plain ringtone I already knew who it was. "Yo, wassup John?" I question, as I picked up phone.

"Shit nothin' major my nigga" he stated. "I was hitting you up to tell you I'm going to scoop you up around twelve."

"Alright my nigga, say no more see you then," I said before we hung up.

"Who was that?" Niniette questioned, as she brought our plates and smoothies out.

"Damn private detective!" I jokingly said.

"Dre, don't get smacked up again," she seriously said.

66

"Damn chill, but it was John telling me he's going to scoop me up around twelve to go hit up the gun range," I stated, as I started tearing up my breakfast.

"Oh O.K, damn nigga that's all you had to say but alright I'll leave after I get done eating," she said. "I need to head back to Atlanta to go show a client that I had to reschedule on this house."

"Why did you have to reschedule?" I curiously questioned, as I finished up my smoothie.

"To come make sure you were all right, Dre" she sincerely said.

"Damn Niniette you didn't have to do all that," I seriously said.

"Dre don't play. You know you mean a lot to me and you know that I will go to war with God behind me over you," she seriously said, as we finished up our food. "Alright Dre, go get ready for what you got going on today. I'll clean up, then go ahead and get outta here." The she grabbed our dishes and leaned over to give me a kiss on the forehead.

I finished up the last of my joint and headed inside and up to my room. I then started up a warm shower and hopped in. Twenty minutes later and I hopped out the shower feeling so good and relaxed. I walked out my bathroom and went in my room to my underwear draw. I grabbed a pair of Calvin Klein boxer briefs and put them on. Then I headed over to my closet to pick out my fit for the day. I started to go through my clothes to see what I wanted to wear. Fuck it, I'll just go plain-Jane. I threw on a black H&M hoodie, black sweatpants, all black Hi-top Air Forces and nice little gold Rolex. My phone then began to ring. "Yo, was up John?" I questioned.

"I'm right outside," he stated before hanging up.

I headed downstairs and out my front door. Then I hopped in my nigga John's whip. "Yo, what's up my nigga?" I questioned, as I hopped in the whip and dapped up with John.

"Shit nothin' major," he replied. "Do you mind if we smoke this OG Kush cigar real quick?"

"Nah my nigga, I'm trying to get blazed anyway," I replied as he lit the cigar and took a huge hit. "

Alright my nigga, so what happened?" he questioned, as he passed me the cigar.

"Alright so I'm at the warehouse checking up on everything and all of a sudden the door gets kicked in," I stated. "Then mad FBI agents start telling me and my workers to get the fuck on the ground." I passed him the cigar. "My ass was still like *what fuck is going on,*" I said. "Then this big buff ass agent scoops me up and slams me on my shit. My nigga I was leaking out the mouth and everything."

"Word my nigga? They did you dirty," he stated.

"Hell yeah my nigga," I replied. "Next thing I know, I see them taking all my shit." He passed me the cigar. "Then one of the agents was like, 'ask him were the cash is at,'" I said, after letting out a bunch of cigar smoke.

"Fuck they wanted to know where your stash was?" he questioned with a serious look as I passed him the cigar.

"My nigga I don't even know," I stated. "But you know I know better than to keep my money and work in the same spot," I said.

"So I was straight on that end but after that, them niggas just bounced," I said as he passed me the cigar back.

"My nigga that shit is wild as fuck," he stated. "But you're going to be happy, I got some good intel for you."

"Oh yeah, I remember you saying that," I replied.

"So what's up with it?" I questioned as I hit the cigar hard as fuck.

"Alright my nigga check this out," he said. "There's this shop called the Native Root Dispensary that sells this exclusive hybrid strain call "Griz Kush". They exclusively grow and sell it, but they were going to fuck with me on a deal. The only issue was the numbers were high. "So I was thinking you could cop it and break me off a piece."

I passed him the cigar. "Shit say no more. Where is this shop at?" I questioned.

"It's in Denver, up in the Aspen mountains," he said.

"O.K I'm fuckin' with it" I said. "When do I need to head down there?"

"That's the catch, tonight" he said.

"TONIGHT? DAMN NIGGA!" I shouted.

"My nigga, it's good," he stated. "I need you to leave tonight because I already booked the flight and hotel. You'll be staying in the five star ski resort called The Little Nell."

"Oh word, you paying? O.K, I'm fuckin' with it," I said, as we dapped hands.

"Alright cool my nigga," he said. "Now let's get up outta here and head over to this gun range." He pulled out from up under my curb and sped off. Twenty minutes later and we pulled up to the gun range. "Alright my nigga, you ready?" John asked.

"Hell yeah nigga!" I expressed with excitement. Then we hopped out his whip and made our way inside. John paid for us to rent three guns. So I picked a Colt 9mm, Desert Eagle and a Mac 10.

"Wise choice, my nigga," he said. "I see how you're trying to play, but I want all the big toys." He picked an AK-47, AR-15 and a M16. After we picked our straps, we headed over to the another room to shoot.

"Hell yeah, this bitch got that serious kick."He said as he started bustin' the M16. I took out my headphones and plugged them up to my phone. Then I started blastin' 21 Savage's song "Red Opps" as I got to bustin' the Mac. After I ran out off bullets I switched guns and songs. I picked up the Colt 9mm and switched to Katie Got Bandz's "Ridin Around & Drillin" as I started to finally shoot all head shots. Last but not least, I shot the Desert Eagle and for that big bitch I blasted Wacka Flacko's "Bustin At Them."

"Alright Dre, you ready?" John asked as he shot his last bullet.

"Hell yeah, once you drop me off I'm about to pack a bag, hop in the shower and head to the airport" I replied.

"That's what I'm talking about," he said. "That raid might of put you on another level of hustlin.'"

We proceeded out the shooting room and exited out the building. We then headed to the parking lot and hopped in his whip. Then we pulled off, back to my spot.

"Alright Dre, text me when you get the work," John said as he pulled up to the curb of my crib.

"Alright bet," I said.

69

I hopped out his whip and made my way to front door. I then immediately headed upstairs to pack my bag and hop in the shower. I was only going to be there for a few days so I packed comfortable and light. Then I packed a few sweatsuits and sneakers and started up a shower. I hopped in my shower, jammin' to "My Savages" by Future. Fifteen minutes later, I hopped out the shower and went in my closet. I threw on my black Versace sweatshirt, black Versace sweatpants, all black pair of 95 Air Max, black Buscemi leather snapback and a gold-tone black face Citizen bracelet watch. Then I grabbed my Snoop Dogg vape pen and 3.5 grams of "Candy Kush" wax. I then packed it in my luggage and headed downstairs to the garage. I threw my luggage in the trunk, hopped in the whip, pulled out the garage and sped off to the airport.

Sixteen minutes later and I pulled up to the car drop off section of the airport. After I dropped my whip off, I headed inside the airport and went through the first class check-in section. Then I headed up the terminal and waited at the gate of my flight. I dipped off to the smoking section of the airport and took out my Snoop Dogg vape pen. I then stuffed a gram of Candy Kush wax into my vape pen and took a couple of hits for the rode. Since I was actually going to Aspen, Colorado I had to fly into Denver first. Then catch another flight from Denver to Aspen. So a couple of hits from my vape pen should have me knocked out until I have to board my second flight.

Just as I took my last hit, my flight was being called. I then rushed back over to the waiting section and made my way onto the plane. I took my first class seat and closed my eyes. Little before I knew it, I was passed out and headed to Denver.

CHAPTER VI

The damn seats were uncomfortable as fuck. I ended up being woken out of my peaceful sleep. The pilots voice came over the intercom telling us to put away all electronic devices and to buckle our seat belts as we were preparing to land. Yes, I woke up just in time, but now I have to spend another three hours on this flight to Aspen. Luckily I have a lot of Candy Kush wax left.

Finally the plane landed in Denver, CO. As soon as the pilot gave us the O.K, I snatched up my carry on luggage and proceeded out the plane. I went to the waiting area of my flight to Aspen. The pilot said it was going to be a thirty minute lay over, so

I went over to the smoking section of the airport. I loaded my Snoop Dogg vape pen with another .5 of Candy Kush wax and proceeded to get faded as fuck. It seem like thirty minutes turned into three hours as I was waiting for my flight to be called. A brother was already dozing off. I took out my headphones, plugged them in to my phone, and played Lil Boosie's new album "Thug Talk" off my Tidal music app. God damn, the first few songs of the album was hot. But before I could get real deep into it, I started to see people making their way to the gate so I grabbed my carry on luggage and headed to the gate.

I made my way through the gate, then into the plane and I took my first class seat. I immediately buckled my seatbelt, closed my eyes and before I knew it I was passed out and on my way to Aspen.

What the fuck, is every seat uncomfortable at these Colorado airports. The uncomfortable seat ended up waking me, in the middle of the plane touching down in Aspen. Finally a nigga is in Aspen.

The pilot O.K'd us to exit the plane, so I grabbed my carry on luggage and dipped out the exit. I then made my way down the terminal and to baggage claim. Finally I snatched my luggage up from baggage claim and headed outside of the airport. There was really no point in me getting a rental, since everything was in walking distance. So I just called a limo service to take me to the hotel. Man this mother fuckin' limo better hurry the hell up, it's cold as fuck out this bitch. A few minutes later and the limo finally pulled up. The driver politely greeted me, then took my luggage. He then put it in the trunk, as I hopped in. Then he peeled outta' Aspen County Airport and headed to my hotel.

Aspen was so mother fuckin' beautiful. All you saw were snowy mountain tops and a bunch of restaurants, hotels and skiers. It was some Disney winter wonderland shit.

A few minutes later and we pulled up to my hotel, "The Little Nell". The driver hopped out, went to the trunk and handed me my luggage. Even though this nigga took forever and a day to pick me up, I still tipped him a fifty. Sometimes you just have to give niggas the benefit of the doubt. I then made my way inside the hotel. I checked into one of their most premier suites called, the "Benedict Suite". After I checked in, I then made my way to the elevator and rode it up to my floor. Then I headed down the hall and into my suite. Immediately after tossing my luggage on the bed, I called the front desk and ordered some dinner. I felt like having some chicken, so I ordered the Roasted Boulder Chicken. It consisted of barley, creme fraiche, red kuri squash and wild mushrooms. I wanted to start my trip of right, so I also ordered a bottle of D'usse. They said it would be ready in about thirty to forty five minutes. So I went to the master bedroom, went through my luggage and got a book I've been meaning to read for a minute now. As I got deep into "The 48 Laws Of Power" by Robert Greene. I really started to rethink a lot of my steps.

Law 28 of the "The 48 Laws Of Power" says to enter with boldness. That is definitely something I needed to master, especially with me about to make these deals tomorrow. Shit if John couldn't get the work at a reasonable price, then I don't really know if there is much I could say. Fuck here I go doubting myself. That raid must of fucked me up, I rarely doubt myself. I should know I'm the shit, I put in more work and time than these other niggas anyway. I always go harder then them, on some Maino shit.

Suddenly I started to hear a knock at the door. Finally my food, a brother is mad hungry. I made my way to the door and grabbed my food. I sat it on the coffee table in the living section of my suite. I grabbed my chromecast flash drive out my luggage, plugged up flash drive to the living room T.V, went YouTube app and played one of my favorite podcast called "Tax Season."

"Yo this nigga Tax is funny as shit" I said to myself, as I poured up some D'usse and dived straight into my dinner. *Man this D'usse definitely has me right,* I thought to myself, as I was still dying laughing from this nigga podcast. By the time I realized I had finished my dinner, I was to fucked up off that D'usse. So there was only thing I could do. I cut off the T.V, went in the master bedroom and got my Snoop Dogg vape pen. Then I stuffed it with a gram of Candy Kush wax. I also took out my Beats Pill and proceeded to the bathroom. I sat my Beats Pill on the counter top and played my favorite album by Drake, "Take Care." Then I proceeded to run some warm, soapy water in the jacuzzi, soaking tub. *Damn this shit feels hell of good,* I thought to myself. I then hopped in the warm, soapy waters of the jacuzzi and relaxed. While fully submerged, I began to take long, smooth hits of the Candy Kush wax smoke. Man being drunk as Hell off D'usse and faded as fuck off this Candy Kush wax, while in this jacuzzi was an amazing feeling. The shit was almost better then the sex I had, with that one girl on my last night in Nicaragua.

This Drake slick had a nigga in his feelings. I mean I'm out here going through all this bullshit with getting raided and losing mad millions. And yeah I'm on vacation, but I still rather be up in this jacuzzi soaking tub with a women comforting me. Nah scratch that, a wife that would not only be comforting me but inspiring me to hustle even harder. Shit am I thinking, what I think I'm thinking. Could I be ready to cut my player ways and settle down. God damn maybe I'm too drunk and not high enough. Or maybe in my fucked up state of mind, I've seem to find some real truth. But who knows, if it's meant for me to find a wife I will receive a sign.

After soaking for a good minute, I decided to head off to bed. I hopped outta' the tub, turned off my Beats Pill and went in the master bedroom. I grabbed a pair of American Eagle boxers, put them on, jumped in bed and passed out sleep.

"Fuck!" I said to myself with a sigh as I woke up at daybreak the next morning. I had a lot of weed to smoke today, so I hopped out of bed and went to the bathroom. Then I started up the warm water from the steam shower.

"Shit, what am I going to wear today?" I said to myself as I walked out the bathroom then into the master bedroom. It was stupid cold in Aspen, so I laid out my grey Ralph Lauren Sport sweat suit and white OVO Jordan 10's. I went back in the bathroom, turned on my Beats Pill, blasting "We Can Freak It" by Kurupt.

Then I hopped in the warm steam shower. The steam shower felt so mother fuckin' good, I was truly relaxed. A few minutes later and I hopped out the shower and headed into the master bedroom. I then got dressed, snatched up my vape pen and my last .5 of Candy Kush wax. Then I made way out my suite. I proceeded down the hall to and the elevator. I hopped on that joint and rode it down to the lobby. Then I headed out the lobby and onto the Aspen streets to go look for a good breakfast spot Two minutes later and I stubble upon this breakfast cafe called, "Poppycock". I liked the vibe there it was nice, chill and very low-key. I then made my way inside and approached the register. I politely greeted the lady at the register and ordered french toast and a strawberry smoothie.

"Hopefully the weed is on point, I need to make bank with it," I said to myself, as I sat down and waited for my food. O.K let's see, the weed shop that I have to go to for John is a couple blocks away. And the weed shop I saw on my way to the hotel, is a block over. So I guess I'll hit up that one first.

"Excuse me sir, your food is ready," the lady at the register said.

Yes finally, I'm hungry as hell, I thought to myself as I grabbed my food and headed outside. Now is the perfect time to smoke some wax. I then reached in my pocket and grabbed my vape pen. I began to smoothly hit it a couple of times.

"Damn this French toast is good as fuck" I said to myself as I began tearing it the fuck up. After I finished my breakfast, I headed over to Green Dragon Aspen dispensary. As I was walking down the cold Aspen streets, I started to think more about settling down. I mean, fuck I'm only twenty-five, is this really something I want to do? Honestly I don't really know what I want to do. I do know I'm tired of waking up in the morning with no woman to cook breakfast for me like Niniette does. At the end if the day a player wants to be loved too. Matter of fact, a player doesn't even want to play the game when he meets a woman that doesn't get played by the game.

"Oh shit I almost missed my turn," I said to myself.

Then I back tracked the block and then proceeded into the weed shop. I politely greeted the lady at the register and ask her to see the manager. The manager came around from the back and to the register, then we immediately chopped it up about business. He told me they had an bomb ass exclusive strain called, "AK Cherry Lime". I didn't have time to test the product right then and there, so along with my thousand seed deal, he also threw in two grams of the strain. See that's how a deal is suppose to go down.

You always should get more then what you pay for. To some people that seems stupid, but you have to think about future business endeavors instead of that one business deal. Now I'm going to definitely come back to shop with him when I need some exclusive shit.

"Shit I feel like Nino Brown in this bitch," I said to myself as I exited the shop. I made my way to the shop John instructed me to go to. It wasn't really that far, more like a couple of blocks over, but that Aspen cold is a different type of cold. I really wanted to go skiing but I had to leave the next day. Plus I can't be relaxed and kickin' back, I'm still in a fucked up position. I wasn't really trippin' about it though. My nigga Ace already told me after we handle or business in Costa Rica and Columbia, our turn up was going to be lit as fuck. Once Ace co-signed a turn up, you just knew the shit was going to be off the wall crazy.

Another block over and I finally made it to "Native Root Dispensary". I made my way inside and immediately saw the manager.

"Hey, how are you doing?" I questioned. "I'm Dre, you spoke with one of my colleagues John about an exclusive strain you guys carry."

"Oh so your the guy John was telling me about," he replied with a raised eyebrow.

"Yes I am" I said.

"The price is a flat four thousand, for a thousand seeds" he boldly stated.

"I understand that, but what I don't understand is why so high?" I curiously questioned.

"Look Dre, I'm not an idiot, I know how y'all get down in Seattle," he sternly replied.

"What do you mean?" I curiously questioned.

"First of all I know you're going to have mad clones and your going to break half of it down to wax and edibles," he stated. "So me charging you four thousand, compared to the tens of thousands your already going to make is light and you know that."

"I'm not going to lie your right, that's exactly what I'm going to do with it," I said.

"I already know, so what's up do we have a deal or not?" he seriously questioned.

"Yes, but I also have a proposal for you," I stated.

"Oh word and what's that?" he curiously questioned.

"I'm about to go see some connects out of Costa Rica and Columbia next week," I said. "So I would like to do a deal with you."

"O.K keep talking, you spiked my interest," he excitingly replied.

"Five hundred seeds for nine hundred dollars," I smoothly stated.

"Nine hundred that's it," he said. "You and I both know your basically just giving five hundred seeds away."

"One could look at it that way, but I choose to look at it like a great way to start off a business relationship" I said.

"You know you what, you're right man, O.K let's do that," he said as he sent one of his workers to go get my seeds.

"Just because you're really fucking with me heavy, I'll throw in seven grams of this strain," he said as we closed the deal.

See that's how you close a mother fuckin' deal, my nigga. No I didn't cop the work for cheaper but I did however spark a nice business relationship. Now when I hit him up for future business endeavors, he knows I'm more beneficial than anything. And that, my friend, will make him more beneficial towards me. Finally I've tied the business up for this trip, now I can fully relax and test all this bud out before I leave tomorrow.

A couple of blocks later and I made it into the hotel. I then headed up the elevator, down the hall and finally into my suite.

"Time to get lifted" I said to myself.

Then I turned on the T.V and listened to some more of the "Tax Season" podcast. First I rolled up a fat ass dutch blunt of the two grams of AK Cherry Lime I had. The AK Cherry Lime was definitely a great high, my body was chill and relaxed as fuck. I know I had stuck gold with this strain, I'm going to flip this shit some many ways. I'll be able to make what I lost in the raid and then some. Next I rolled up seven joints of the seven grams of Griz Kush that I picked up from other dispensary. Man by the third joint, I was already higher than a giraffe's ass. I wanted to stop right there, but I had four more joints left. So I just kept smoking and listening to this funny ass nigga Tax. Man I'm glad they gave a street nigga his own podcast, finally they gave a street nigga a platform where he can talk his shit. Not too much into laughing at that nigga and I tapped out on joint number five.

"What the fuck?!" I said to myself as daybreak woke me up the next morning. Shit, I didn't think that Griz Kush would have me knocked the fuck out like that.

I checked the time. God damn it's 8:30, fuck, I have to catch my flight at eleven. I hopped up off the couch. I then called the hotel and ordered belgian style waffles and the little nell omelette. There omelette consistent of seasonal mushrooms, goat cheddar and braised kale with a freshly squeezed orange juice. After I ordered my food I went into the master bedroom and laid out my outfit. Then I packed up the rest of my luggage. I went into the bathroom, started up my shower, got undressed and hopped in. My re-up game had been all the way on point, due to this trip. Soon as I touched back down in Seattle, I was going to head straight to the warehouse and drop this work off. This shit needed to grow fast, but I wasn't going to put that type of pressure on my growers. If the love and care of the plant isn't right, then it's just not going to smoke right.

"Ok that's enough of this steam," I said to myself. I then hopped out the shower and went into the master bedroom to get dressed. Soon as I finished getting dressed I started to hear a knock at the door, finally my breakfast was here. I made my way to the door and snatched up my breakfast. Then I sat in the living section and got faded off the last two joints I had. I turned on the TV and watched Dame Dash's YouTube channel "Hip Hop Motivation."

Man this nigga Dame spits nothing but priceless jewels. In business, it's really about putting up your own money if you want to truly be considered the boss. Other then that, you're just a nigga supervising someone else's money. Sometimes that's just how the game goes though, I often have to make deals with mangers instead of owners. That's why I fuck with my nigga Ace. He's the type of nigga to take you straight to the connect, fuck all that middle man shit. After finishing my breakfast I called the limo service to pick me up and take me to the airport. Then I packed up my Beats Pill and chromecast flash drive and proceeded out the door. Then down the hall and onto the elevator and made my way down to the lobby and I checked in my room key. "Hopefully this limo isn't late like last time," I said to myself, as I made way out the hotel.

I then saw my limo pulling right up. The driver hopped out, politely greeted me, and put my luggage in the trunk. He hopped back in the car and pulled off toward the airport. Twenty minutes later and we pulled up to Aspen Country Airport. The driver hopped out and got my luggage out the trunk. I politely thanked him for his services and tipped him a fifty. "Hopefully that made his day," I said to myself. I entered into the airport and proceeded to go through first class luggage check-in. Man I love first class; I quickly made it through luggage check-in. I then made my down terminal and waited at the gate of my flight. As I'm waited for my flight, my phone began to ring. I saw the caller ID. A New York number?

"Oh shit I know who this is," I said to myself as I picked up the phone.

"Wassup Alicia, what's good with you?" I excitingly questioned.

"Hey Dre, I'm fine how about you?" she questioned.

"I've seen better days, but overall I'm good," I replied.

"That's great to hear," she said. "Dre, I have ask you something."

"What's up?" I questioned.

"Can you fly out to New York, I want to see you?" she questioned.

"Sure," I stated. "I have some business to take care of next week, so that following week I got you."

"Alright Dre, you promise?" she seriously questioned.

"Word is bond, I got you," I said as my flight was being called. "Look I got to go, but most definitely I'm going to make that happen."

"Alright Dre, see you then," she said before we both hung up.

"Man these females are a trip," I said to myself as I boarded my flight and took my seat.

I fell asleep before the plane could even took off to Denver. A few hours later and the roughness of the plane's landing woke me up. "Finally we're in Denver," I said to myself as I began to

79

yawn.

The pilot gave us the green light to exit the plane, so I picked up my carry luggage and proceeded out the plane. Since we had a thirty minute layover, I decided to catch up on some new music. I went to my mixtape app Spinrilla and listened to Blac Youngsta's new mixtape "Young & Reckless." I saw the big homie on "The Breakfast Club" counting damn near a quarter million in cash. Ever since I seen that, I definitely had to fuck with the kid. You know how the saying goes, real recognizes real and I definitely recognize a real get money ass nigga when I see one. Not too much into listening to this bomb ass tape and I already saw people boarding the plane. I hopped up and snatched up my carry-on luggage, then proceeded to board the plane. "Hopefully I can fall back asleep," I said to myself, as I took my seat on the plane. I closed my eyes just a little bit after take off and I eventually fell asleep.

"Excuse me, sir," a stewardess said, while tapping me on the shoulder. I opened my eyes. She told me we had just landed and that I could exit the plane.

"Yes now I'm back in the city, time to get my paper right," I said to myself.

I got up, stretched and grabbed my carry-on luggage, then made my way off the plane. I headed all the way down the terminal and then to baggage claim. I picked up the rest of my luggage and headed outside to the car drop off section to pick up my whip. While putting my luggage in the trunk I still couldn't help but think of what Alicia wanted to see me for. It sounded really important, but then again she could just want a brother to drop that lumber one time for the one time.

I hopped in the whip, pulled out of the airport and sped off to my warehouse. Traffic was pretty light, so I made it to my warehouse pretty quick. Hopefully shit isn't too fucked up. I told my head grower to tell everyone else to clean up, but I never got a chance to check everything out. I pulled up to my warehouse and parked up on the curb.

"Yo, was up Dre?" my head grower question. I then popped the trunk, hopped out and got the seeds from both strains out my luggage.

"What's good, bruh?" I said as I shut the trunk and dapped him up.

"Please tell me you got some good news, the guys and I have been worried," he stated.

"I definitely have some great news" I said.

"O.K, so wassup?" he questioned.

"Wassup is I picked up two exclusive strains from outta Aspen," I stated.

"Oh word?" he excitingly said.

"Hell yeah, my nigga I smoked both these shits myself and this is definitely some high quality shit," I said. I handed him brown paper bags with the seeds in glass containers.

"O.K I see you, that's definitely what's up" he happily said.

"You already know, but fuck all that how is the warehouse looking?" I questioned.

"Everything is cleaned up," he stated.

"We already started spouting the seeds for all the plants that were snatched up," he said.

"Oh word, that's wassup my nigga," I stated."I most certainly have to raise y'all pay for holding everything down."

"Dre you already know you have a six star squad, so you shouldn't expect anything less," he said

"You're most definitely right but I'm about to get up outta here," I stated. "I'll be back around in another week to drop some more work off."

"Alright bet," he said. Then we dapped up and I hopped back in my car and sped off back to my crib.

The sky started to clear up, as I was speeding down the freeway. So I dropped the top then blasted my favorite song by Blac Youngsta: "Druglord." A few minutes later and I was pulling into my garage. I popped the trunk as I pulled all the way in. Then I hopped out, snatched up my luggage and proceeded inside. As I was heading upstairs I dialed up my nigga Ace, so I could get the details on our trip.

"Yo wassup my guy?" I questioned as he answered the phone.

"Shit nothin', I was actually just about to hit you up but you beat me to it," he stated.

"Aye man you know I have to up my hustle, so I'm pressin'

shit hard," I said. "I just got back from Aspen today."

"I heard that my nigga you gotta' get your paper right," he said. "Oh yeah, book your flight for Costa Rica today cause I'm leaving the day after tomorrow."

"Alright I'm packing my shit now, oh and where are we going to be staying and how long?" I questioned.

"We're going to be staying at the Four Seasons Resort Costa Rica at Peninsula Papagayo, and for one day and two nights," he stated. "The connect is going to meet us at our suite as soon as we get there. Then after we finish business you know we're going to go have some fun. Then after our two days are up, we're going to catch a flight to Colombia."

"Alright, shit I like the sound of that," I stated.

"Do you want me to book the flight to Colombia?" I questioned.

"Nah I already booked our flight for Colombia, plus the hotels for Costa Rica and Colombia," he stated. "All you have to do is book the flight for Costa Rica. And book the flight for an early morning one, I don't want to keep the connect waiting."

"Alright bet, I got you my nigga," I said."I'm going to book my flight right now."

"Alright bruh, I'll see you in Costa Rica the day after tomorrow then," he said.

"You already know" I said before we both hung up."Shit I forgot to call John" I said to myself after I wrapped up my convo with Ace. "Yo, was up my nigga?" I questioned, as he answered the phone.

"Shit nothin' just kickin', pimpin' and trippin,'" he said with a chuckle.

"My nigga, yo ass sound high as shit," I said with a chuckle.

"Hell yeah, this Khalifa Kush got my ass higher than the moon, but fuck all that, what's good with the business?" he questioned.

"Everything went perfect my nigga" I stated. "I scored the work and I'll break you off when my growers get to drying the bud." Then I went in my closet and grabbed 3.5 grams of Mango Kush and a honey berry backwood.

"Alright bet, that's what's up," he said.

"Yo my nigga, I almost forgot to tell you, that girl from Nicaragua hit me up today," I said. I headed downstairs to the kitchen to whip me up something to eat.

"Oh word, what was she talking about?" he questioned.

"Shit, nothin' major," I said. "She just wanted to know if I could fly over to New York, so she can see me." I took out some fresh jumbo shrimp and crab legs.

"Damn my nigga she's that hooked on you?" he questioned.

"I guess so my nigga, shit you drop that lumber the right way and they will come crawling back," I said.

Then I began to season my shrimp and crab. I put the shrimp back in the fridge to marinate and threw the crab legs in a huge pot to cook at a boil.

"Fuck you think, you're a pimp?" he jokingly questioned.

"Naw nigga I'm mac mother fuckin' Daddy Dre nigga!" I jokingly expressed.

"Well alright mac mother fuckin' Daddy Dre" he said, as we both busted out laughing.

"Boy you stupid, but I'm going to hit you up later, a brother is cooking" I stated.

"Alright my nigga, stay up," he said.

"You to my nigga," I said before we both hung up.

Shit what do I feel like watching? I sat in front of my kitchen TV and began to unroll my backwood. I dumped the tobacco and stuffed it with the 3.5 grams of Mango Kush. I finally decided what I wanted to watch, so I went to my YouTube app on my kitchen T.V and played my favorite web series: "Money & Violence."

"Shit I'm mad thirsty," I said to myself.

I then walked over to my wine cellar and grabbed a bottle of Bel Air rosé champagne and poured up a half of glass. Thirty minutes later and my crab legs were almost done so I took my marinated jumbo shrimp out the fridge and my homemade cannabutter. I don't really use cannabutter like that, it takes so much weed and butter to make another batch. Plus it gets me way too fucked up when I use it to infuse my meals. But tonight I'm trying to get fucked up.

Twenty minutes later and I was plating my cannabis

infused jumbo shrimp and crabs. I then took my food, bottle of rosé Bel Air champagne and glass and headed into the living room. Shit what do I want to watch? I went through my movies off my Netflix app.

"Oh Hell yeah, this is my shit," I said to myself. Then I played one of my favorite movies starring DMX: "Never Die Alone."

Man "Never Die Alone" is one of my favorite movies, it's about standing on principal and nothing is more gangster than a man righting his wrongs and paying his debts. A man's word is his bond and if a man brakes his word, then in certain worlds, different things can happen. But in the hood it usually results in death and when death has to happen, you must take a man's life in a honorable way. Fuck I'm high as Hell — like really high. I was so fucked up off smoking a whole 3.5 and eating my cannabis infused meal that I just passed out on the couch.

A day later and I was awoken by my five-am alarm. I had to wake up mad early, since I scheduled my flight for 6:30 a.m. I know that's early as fuck, but it is a ten hour flight with a three hour layover in Atlanta. I'm going to need eight brownies and three cookies for this trip.

I hopped out of bed and walked over to my closet, to pick out my fit. Since it was going to be mad hot when I touched down in Costa Rica, I laid out my white Gucci polo shirt with the green & red stripes on the collar, tan H&M slacks and white Versace loafers to match. After I laid out my fit I went to my bathroom and started me up a nice warm shower. Fourteen minutes later I hopped out, got dressed, snatched up my luggage and headed downstairs to my kitchen. I didn't feel like having an actual meal so I blended up some strawberries, raspberries, blueberries, pineapples slices, kiwis slices and kale. Then I heated up two of my homemade cinnamon apple pop-tarts.

"Shit I got to go," I said to myself, as the clock had just hit 5:45 a.m.

I then proceeded out my kitchen, pass the living room and into the garage. I hopped in the whip, tossed my luggage in the back, pulled out my garage and sped off to the airport. Finally I'm going to be back in trying tropics, just what the fuck I need. I already knew me and Ace were about to be lit.

A few minutes later and I pulled up to the airport. I then dropped my whip off in the car drop off section. Then I hopped out, snatched up my luggage from the backseat, and proceeded into the airport. I got my luggage and shit checked in mad fast, since had a first class ticket. I headed down the terminal and already people were boarding the flight, so I lightly jogged and made it just in time.

"Yes I made it," I said to myself as I boarded the plane and took my seat. "Now it's time to get high, while I get high."

I then took out half of a weed brownie, ate it and closed my eyes as the plane took off heading to Atlanta.

CHAPTER VII

"God damn this plane is landing rough as fuck," I grumpily said to myself as I felt the plane land. But fuck it, now I'm finally in Atlanta.

The pilot came over the intercom telling us we could unbuckle our seat belts and then exit the plane. For some reason I just plugged in my earphones and played Kid Cudi's song "Day & Night." At that point I know I was way too fucked up off the brownie. Man this song had me trippin' hard, so I decided to switch vibes and watch mad episodes of one of my favorite series "The Boondocks." A couple of hours passed by slowly as I watched a few episodes of "The Boondocks." Just one more hour then I'll be back in the beautiful blue sky's and on my way to Costa Rica.

Then one hour turned into thirty minutes and at that point I decided to go ahead and pop a cookie so I could already be fucked up and passed out exactly when I took my seat on the plane. *Damn that cookie was starting to kick the fuck in,* I thought to myself just as my flight was being called to board. I snatched up my carry on luggage and proceeded to board my flight. Once I got on the plane I immediately took my seat and looked out the window. The sun was so bright and the beautiful baby blue sky had little bubbly clouds sporadically spreading all across. Man I'm really fucked up but I love this feeling; I love my life even though bullshit happens, at least I was gifted time to fix it.

As the the plane took off in the sky, I decided to close my eyes and take off into some sleep until I woke up in Liberia, Costa Rica.

"Damn the sun is bright as fuck," I said to myself as I began to wake up just as we were preparing to land.

Everything felt different in Costa Rican atmosphere. The sun shone brighter, the clouds were bigger and fluffier, and the sky seemed like a even more shiner baby blue.

A few minutes after landing and the pilot instructed us to unbuckle or seat belts and exit the plane. I then unbuckled my seat belt, hopped up, grabbed my carry on luggage and exited the plane. Once I got off the plane, I made my way down the terminal to baggage claim. I snatched up the rest of my luggage. I headed out the airport to catch my shuttle to the resort. As soon as I stepped outside I saw the shuttle waiting for me. Now that's what I'm talking about, my late ass needed that — it was already 7:25 p.m. By the time I got to the resort, the only thing we were going to be able to do was make the deal and go out to a bar. I put my luggage in the trunk of the shuttle and hopped in. While riding to the resort I just took in the chill vibes of Costa Rica.

Everything felt at peace, you know just one with nature. But for some reason I was still feeling some type of way. Maybe I just need to make this deal and turn up a bit, then my spirits should be where they need to be.

Damn this resort is mad beautiful. It was like a resort hidden in the high trees on the coast of Costa Rica. The driver then pulled up to the entrance of the lobby. He popped the trunk so I could get my luggage. I hopped out, went around to the trunk, and snatched up my luggage. I tipped the driver a twenty before he pulled off. The lobby of the resort was really different than any other hotels and resorts I've stayed in. It was very open and colorful with a nice floral design on the walls and beautiful stone pillars.

"Damn this nigga Ace got us a suite on the private residence side of the resort," I said to myself after I checked-in at the lobby.

One of the workers brought around a golf cart for me to use so I could drive over to the private residence side of the resort.

"YO DRE, WHAT TOOK YOU SO FUCKIN' LONG?" Ace shouted from the balcony as I pulled up to our private residence.

"My nigga Ace!" I said, as I got up to the door of our residence.

"Dre, what's good?" Ace questioned as we dapped up.

"Yo, this shit is amazing, my nigga," I said as I looked around at the house.

"YO PUT YOUR STUFF IN THE OTHER ROOM, I'M ABOUT TO HIT UP MY CONNECT!" he shouted from the main room.

I went to go put my luggage in the other room. The room that I was in was truly amazing. It had a dope ass view of the Pacific Ocean and a private entrance that I didn't even notice till now.

"Yo Ace how did you find this resort my guy?" I questioned. "This shit is mad dope."

I walked into the living room.

"I know my nigga, but don't get comfortable, you know we're leaving tomorrow morning," he stated.

"Hell yeah, I got to get the rest of this work nigga," I said.

All of a sudden we start to hear a knock at the door.

"I got it Dre, it's the connect," Ace said as he got up to answer the door.

"How are you doing fellas?" the connect questioned as he entered through the door with an all black Fendi leather briefcase.

"We're good," Ace said.

"You can take a seat over there," Ace said as they walked back over to living room.

I was really surprised by this dude's style. I've never seen a Hispanic dude that has tattoos all over his neck and arms, dress business casual before.

"So this is what I have for you gentlemen," the connect said, as he popped open his briefcase.

"GOD DAMN!" I shouted, as he popped open the briefcase. The smell of finely grown marijuana hit me in my shit like a mother fuckin' Jon Jones punch.

"Yes I know, this is Costa Rica's finest right here," the connect said. "It doesn't get any better then this."

"I hear you talkin' and you definitely have the interest of my partner, but what are the numbers hittin' for?" Ace questioned.

"Ace, you come highly recommended and your partner's enthusiasm really makes me comfortable," the connect said. "How about three bands for four thousand seeds, plus I'll throw in seven grams of this shit as a thank you."

"Wow you're being real generous today," Ace said.

Then we both took out our cards and swiped it off his e-card reader.

"It's not about generosity, it's about the connection," the connect said. "If I hit you off with a great deal now, later on down the line you're going to fuck with me on an even greater deal."

"You're right about that, we'll definitely be in touch," Ace said as the connect handed us our packages.

"I'll definitely be expecting your call," the connect said.

Then he stood up and made his way out the door.

"Yo real rap, that Hispanic nigga is cool as fuck," I said.

"Hell yea, my Intel on the best connects are always on point," Ace said.

"Shit nigga you ain't never lied," I stated.

"Yo Dre, I heard the bar at this resort stays lit at this time of night," he stated.

"So what are you tryin' to do?" he questioned.

"Nigga do you even have to ask, lets hit the spot up," I happily said.

"Alright cool, let's put this work up and then we can dip," he said.

"Alright say no more," I said.

Then we both got up and headed to our rooms to put the seeds away. Before we left, Ace rolled up a fat ass blunt of the Costa Rican bud we just coped.

"Bru this shit is sticky as fuck, my nigga!" he expressed as he finished rolling up.

"That's what I'm talking about!" I stated.

We then made our way to the door, outside and onto the lounge and bar of the resort.

"Damn bruh, this is some good bud," I stated as I started coughing like fuck.

"Nigga I know, yo ass is about to die out this bitch," he said as we approached the lounge.

"Oh this shit is lit," I stated as we started hearing merengue music.

"Let's sit towards the beach view tables so we can peep the vibe," he said.

The we headed to the beach view tables and called over a waiter.

We had the munchies like fuck so we just ordered their House Burger, which consisted of caramelized onions, Swiss cheese bacon and crispy potato wedges.

"Yo my nigga it's some fine, jawns out this joint," I stated.

"Hell yeah, I might just have to pick up two of them," he said.

"Nigga, you ain't no mac," I said as our waiter brought our food over.

"Nigga who ain't no mac? Dre you already know how I play," he said as we both started eating.

"Alright whatever nigga, you know I was the man back in those University days," he said.

"Shit I'm not even goin' to lie, you were pullin' the baddies with the fatties back in the day," I said as I finished up my burger.

"You already know and speaking of fatties, do you see those two big booty sisters staring a brother down?" he questioned.

"You talkin' about the two women with the fishtail braids sitting at the bar," I questioned as Ace began wiping his hands and face with a napkin.

"Hell yea, I'm about to run game," Ace said as he got up.

"You better think your a mac like me nigga," I jokingly stated.

"Fuck all that, I'm about to have me a Ménage à trois with some real sisters," he jokingly stated.

As Ace left to run game on the two big booty baddies at the bar, I noticed a fine ass light brown Hispanic chick, just low-key in the cut sippin' on some bubbly. I checked my breath, my nose and nails, yes nails, y'all know females hate a nigga with some dirty nails.

"Damn I hope she doesn't diss a nigga" I said to myself. Then I got up and began walking over to her. "Hey how are you doing beloved?" I questioned with a smile as she looked up at me with her beautiful almond-shaped greenish color eyes.

"I'm fine," she stated with a smile as I sat down.

"I'm not even goin' to lie to you, I'm heavily attracted to your demeanor," I flirtatious said.

"Oh really now," she said. "What's your game plan, buy me a couple of drinks and take me back to your suite to fuck?" she boldly questioned as she sipped her champagne.

"I was really hoping to explore your mind a little bit while I buy myself some drinks," I said. "But I'll take your vision into consideration."

"Explore my mind while you buy yourself some drinks, how about we make the feeling mutual?" she questioned with a smile as she called over a waiter. "What do you drink, brown or white?"

"Brown, preferably D'usse," I said as the waiter came over.

"Can I get a double shot of Apple Ciroc?" she asked the waiter.

"Oh I see how you're trying to play," I stated. "Can I also get a double shot of D'usse?"

The waiter then told us that he'll be back with our drinks shortly.

"I never did get your name beloved," I stated.

"No names, no ages, just strangers on vacation getting drunk," she replied as the waiter came back with our drinks.

"I like that answer," I said as we both knocked down our first shot.

After chopping it up about sex, drugs, and love, we downed our second shots and ordered another round. Man shorty could drink her mother fuckin' ass off. We ordered up another round and somewhere between the fifth and sixth shot, she stood up and sat in my lap. Then she whispered in my ear that she wanted me to explore something else. So I automatically picked her up and then headed back to her suite.

"Damn, what the fuck," I said to myself as I woke up in the bed of a beautiful light brown Hispanic shorty with a fat ass. *Oh yeah, that did happen,* I thought to myself as I remembered leaving the lounge with shorty last night.

See that's why I rarely drink white liquor, I barely remember shit when I wake up the next morning. I got up grabbed my clothes, got dressed and bounced. Damn man, this trip has been wild already and we haven't even made it to Colombia. I was still excited to be heading to New York the day after I got back from Colombia though. I headed up the stairs and unlocked the gate to the private entrance of my room.

"YO DRE IS THAT YOU!" Ace shouted from the other room.

"AYE NIGGA, COME UP IN HERE IM ROLLING UP!" he shouted.

I grabbed my Beats Pill and headed into living room. After, I sat down and started to blast a lot Migos. We didn't really talk much. I could tell he was tired as fuck, so we just let the music vibe us out.

"Alright bru I'm about to pack my luggage, take a shower and get dressed," he said. "We're about to have breakfast then head over to the airport."

"Bet," I said. We got up and headed into our rooms.

Fuck what do I want to wear? I went through my luggage and took out my grey Balmain hoodie, grey Ralph Lauren and grey & black Yeezy Boast 350's.

"Damn this shower is relaxing as hell" I said to myself as I hopped in the shower. Fourteen minutes later I hopped out the shower, got dressed and snatched up my luggage. Then I headed to the living room, packed up my Beats Pill and waited for Ace.

"Aye bru do you got a vape pen on you?" he questioned as he walked in the living room with all his luggage.

"Yeah," I replied.

"Alright cool, here is the rest of this Costa Rican bud," he said as he handed me the sack. Before we left I stuffed the rest of the bud in my Snoop Dogg vape pen.

"You done bruh?" he questioned.

"Yeah I'm done" I stated.

Then we packed up the golf cart with our luggage and drove it down to the breakfast spot of the resort. We parked up on the curb, hopped out and took our ocean view seats. A waiter immediately came over as we took our seats. I then ordered their Latin special, Chicken Tamales, and Ace ordered a regular eggs and bacon type of breakfast.

"Alright my nigga, lets get into it," I stated. "What the actual fuck happened last night?" I questioned, as took out my vape pen and began to slowly hit it.

"My nigga, it went all the way the fuck down. I'm not going to speak on it to much but they were definitely real sisters," he said with a grin as I passed him the vape pen.

"What about you my nigga I seen you running game on a bad one last night," he said as our food arrived.

"My nigga I was so fucked up off that Apple Ciroc, all I remember is taking shorty to her room," I said as I was tearing up my food.

"So did you smash my nigga?" Ace questioned as he passed me my vape pen and started eating.

"I'm pretty sure I did since we both woke up ass naked," I said as I finished up my food. "Aye bruh, I'm going to go ahead and pay for the food."

92

"Cool, I should be done when you get back," he said as he was finishing up his meal.

I then headed over to the bar section, paid our bill and tipped our waiter a fifty before I walked back over to our table.

"Alright Dre, I'm ready" he stated. "Lets check out the resort and head over to the airport so we can start over journey to Columbia."

We walked over to the golf cart and rode it down to the lobby.

Damn I had a dope ass time here, I thought to myself as Ace checked in both our room keys at the front desk.

"I just told the hotel to get us a limousine to the airport so it should be here momentarily," he said as he walked backed over to the golf cart.

Ten minutes later and the limo pulls up. The limo driver hopped out and helped us load our luggage from the golf cart and into his trunk. We then all hopped in and he peeled off toward Daniel Quiros International airport. Thirty minutes later and we had finally arrived at the airport. The driver popped the trunk, got out and helped us with our luggage. I politely thanked him then tipped him a fifty. Ace and I then headed inside the airport and went to our first class luggage check-in. After we got all of our luggage checked in, we headed down the terminal and waited at the gate of our flight.

"Dre, did you bring the edibles?" he questioned.

"Hell yeah, you trying to pop one now?" I questioned.

"Yes my nigga, I need to be knocked out on this flight and for the layover in Atlanta," he said.

"Shit I feel you bruh," I said.

Then I went in my carry-on luggage and gave Ace half of a Sour Diesel brownie.

"Good lookin,'" he said, as our flight was being called.

We then boarded the plane and took our first class seats. Ace was already knocked out as soon as we sat down. So I popped the other half of the brownie and closed my eyes as the plane took off to Atlanta.

"Dre," Ace said as he kept pushing my shoulder.

"Wassup bruh?" I questioned as I began to open my eyes.

"We're here bruh," Ace said as he stood up to grab his carry

93

on luggage. I then did the same and we both made our way off the plane and into the waiting section for our flight to Bogota, Colombia.

"Aye bruh, do we still have some more bud left in your vape pen?" he questioned.

"Yeah we have a nice little amount," I said.

"Alright let's go over to the smoking section real quick," he said. "I need to be passed out for this four hour layover."

A few puffs later and we were high as fuck. I'm pretty sure the people in the smoking section knew we weren't smoking tobacco, since our eyes were red as fuck and we kept laughing mad hard.

"Alright Dre I'm high and know I'm about to go pass out in a corner somewhere," he stated as we headed back to the waiting section.

Ace went over to a nice little corner in the waiting section and passed the fuck out while a couple of hours of me not doing shit went by. I decided to check "The Breakfast Club" to see if they had some new shit up. *P. Diddy shit this should be a cool ass interview,* I thought to myself as I plugged in my headphones and played the interview. Damn man, this nigga really has his own charter school, that is really inspirational to me. I think I need to look into getting my own charter school and putting it on the south side of Chicago. Sometimes I get all wrapped up in the five star hotels, designer clothes, fast cars and fancy jewelry. I end forgetting, that I have a personal responsibility to give knowledge, opportunities and resources to my people.

As soon as I finished watching the interview our flight was being called to board. I snatched up my carry on luggage, woke Ace up, and we boarded our flight. Ace automatically went back to sleep as we took our first class seats. I took out a half of a OG Kush cookie, ate it and closed my eyes as our plane took off and headed to Bogota, Colombia.

"Yo Dre, Dre," Ace said as I started to open my eyes. "We just landed."

Then he stood up and grabbed his carry on luggage. I did the same, as I started to fully wake up for my oh so great sleep. We then exited from the plane, made our way down the terminal and snatched up our luggage from baggage claim. Then we headed out the airport and waited for the shuttle service.

"Ace this shit is amazing," I said in amazement as I started taking in the weather.

"I know my nigga, I wish we were going to be here longer than two days," he said. "I would of took you over Medina to check Pablo Escbor's crib."

"Shit don't even worry about it, we'll definitely vacation here when I'm not pressed for time," I said, as the shuttle pulled up.

The driver politely greeted us as he hooped out and helped us put our luggage in the trunk. We all then hopped back in and the driver peeled out the airport and off to Four Seasons Hotel Medina Bogota. Forty minutes later and we pulled up to the hotel. The driver popped the trunk hopped out and helped us with our luggage. I then tipped him a fifty for his services just before he pulled off.

"Damn the Four Seasons always has some dope hotels, I need to buy some of their stock," I said as we entered the hotel. Ace checked us in, then we headed upstairs through the elevator and down the hall to our suite.

"Damn, what the fuck!" I said as we entered into a big ass suite.

"Yeah nigga, what you thought this was?" He questioned. "You know I had to book the the penthouse suite. AYE BRUH, I'M ABOUT TO HIT THE CONNECT," he shouted from the other room.

Then I headed into the other room and put my luggage up.

"I just got off the phone with him, he said he'll be here in twenty minutes" he said as he came back in the living room.

"Alright say no more," I said, and then we got to talking about all kinds of bullshit. "Yo Ace you are a mother fuckin' fool," I said while dying laughing at this nigga telling me a story of how he fucked some nigga girl in Paris. Then all of a sudden, we start to hear a knock at the door.

"I got it Dre, it's the connect" he said as he hopped up and went to open the door. Then both Ace and the connect came into the living room and sat down.

What's up with these tatted, up well dress Hispanic connects, I thought to myself as the connect popped open his suite case.

"WOW!" I shouted in amazement of how green the bud was, plus it was heavy in crystals, which my clients would like a lot.

"Yes I know, very impressive," the connect said in his Spanish accent.

"Yes it is very impressive but what are the numbers like?" Ace seriously questioned.

"Five thousand seeds each for thirty-five hundred US dollars" the connect said.

"Those are some great numbers don't you think Dre?" Ace questioned.

"Yes they are, but how much for a seven grams of this bud?" I questioned.

"For you, eighty dollars," the connect said.

"Shit that's was up, lets do the deal then," I said. Then Ace and I took out our cards and swiped them on the connects e-card reader.

"Before I go, I heard why they call you Ace, so here's two bottles of Ace Of Spade for you gentlemen," the connect said. Then he grabbed the bottles out of a bag I didn't notice he had with him before.

"Thanks my dude," Ace said, as he shook the connects hand and let him out. "Alright my nigga we've made the deal, now let's go get something to eat," Ace said to me

We put our work up and headed out of the suite, down the hall, to the elevator and got off at the lobby then headed outside.

"Yo Dre, I know a good spot we can get something to eat at," he stated. "It's a few blocks from a college, so it might be some fine Columbians that we can run game on."

"Shit that's wassup, let's head over there then," I said as we headed down the block. As we were walking down the block, I started to really peep the chill warm vibe of Columbia — everything was quite relaxing.

"Alright here we are, La Vercinda Mexican Grill," he said as we then made our way inside.

We were politely greeted as we took our seats. A waiter then immediately came over to give us menus. I took a look at the menu and ordered some seafood fajitas and a lemonade. Ace ordered the same, then the waiter said he'd be back with our order. A few minutes later and the waiter came back with our seafood fajitas and lemonades.

"Yo Dre" Ace said as I started tearing up my food.

"Wassup bru?" I questioned.

"Peep those two fine ass Colombians in the back corner," he said.

"God damn shorty is bad, I want the dark skin one with the ass bustin' out her leggings," I said.

"Say no more, as soon as we finish eating we're definitely on that," he said.

"Alright Ace, are you ready my nigga?" I questioned as we finished up.

"Hell yeah," he said.

Then we got up and made our way over to there table. We got over to their table and immediately started running game. Ace was running game on the brown skin Columbian and she was hell of bad. She had nice long, thick hair, a nice ass little booty and a pretty ass face, but the one I had was badder. I've never seen a dark skin Colombian before, but she was like queen. I'm talking about long straight hair, falling down to her big ass booty and plus she had a pretty ass face. A few more minutes of running game and they were ready to head back to the hotel. We paid for our meal and there's, then we all headed out of the restaurant and made our way back to the hotel.

A couple of blocks later we approached the hotel then headed inside. We made our way to the elevator, rode it up to our level and hopped out. Then we headed down the hall and into the suite. Ace and I didn't waste anytime trying to get them up in our rooms. They already knew what type of situation this was, so Ace took his girl to his room and I did the same.

"Do you smoke?" I questioned.

I then took out the seven grams of Colombian bud I just copped and some sheets of tobacco leaves out my luggage.

"Yeah, a little bit," she said. Then she kicked off her shoes and hopped on the bed to watch me roll up a marijuana cigar.

"I'm about to go run us a bath," I said as I finished rolling up. Then I grabbed my cigar, bottle of Ace and my Beats Pill out my luggage and headed into the bathroom. I started up a nice, warm soapy bath and set my Beats Pill on the marble countertop, blasting Miguel's album "All I Want Is You."

"BRING YO FINE ASS UP IN HERE!" I shouted from the bathroom as I poured her up a glass of Ace Of Spade. Then I lit my Colombian weed filled cigar, just as she walked in with her beautiful, butt naked Colombian ass.

"I know, mesmerizing right?" she questioned.

Then she took my cigar out my hands and took a long hit before sat it down on the ashtray by the tub. Then she proceeded to undress me. I slipped in the tub while grabbing the bottle of Ace Of Spades and my cigar. Then she slipped on top of me and grabbed her glass and we toasted up. Shorty downed her whole glass, took the bottle out my hand and started gulping that bitch. We definitely had some surfboard action going on, as I was getting the bathroom mad smokey. I was straight hot boxin' that bitch. After I smoked the cigar down half way, we hopped out the tub and headed back in my room. I took my baby oil out my luggage and we oiled each other down. We hopped back in bed and, from that point, the rest was history.

The next morning I woke up at day break. Man last night was wild. I still couldn't believe how shorty just bounced like that right after we were done.

I hopped out of bed and went to my luggage to lay out my fit. I checked the weather app on my phone and saw that it was sunny and but still windy in Seattle. So I laid out my black and white Hyper Elite Nike jacket, black Nick tech sweatpants and black and white Nike Cortez sneaks. Then I headed in the bathroom and started up my shower. I still couldn't help but think of shorty dipped out last; it's like she already knew how the game went. But I wasn't really trippin', she definitely played her position.

Fifteen minutes later and I hopped out the shower and headed back in the room. I got dressed, packed up my luggage and took it to the door of the hotel. Ace was already chillin' on the couch, all dressed and ready.

"Yo Ace I'm ready, but let's smoke this half cigar I have left," I stated. I went back in the room to grab the half of cigar and a lighter. "Alright my nigga lets get lifted" I said as I came back to the living room.

I then coped a squat on the couch and proceeded to light up and smoke up. Man we were smoking that bitch for at least twenty minutes strong. After we got down to the a long roach I put it out, so we could head out for breakfast and then to the airport. We snatched up our luggage, headed out the door and down the hall to the elevator. We rode down to the lobby and walked around to restaurant of the hotel.Then we sat down and were politely greeted by a waiter handing us menus. I proceeded to order the panfried salmon and Ace ordered grilled shrimp.

"Yo, so what happened last night?" he questioned as the waiter left.

"Nothin' major, I had shorty up in the tub getting drunk as hell off the Ace," I said. "What about you, my nigga?"

"Shit you already know how I rock," Ace said.

"O.K, I hear you talkin'," I said as the waiter came back with our food. "Man I can't wait to get back home, I'm about to head out tomorrow," I stated, while attacking the hell out my food.

"Damn Dre, you're about to go make some more plays without a brother," Ace said.

"Nah, it's not even that type of party. I'm about to go see one of my constituents outta New York" I said as we started to finish up our breakfast.

"O.K I see you, already know what type of trip that is," he said. "Her box better be A1." He finished up his drink.

"Something like that, but fuck all that, are you ready my nigga?" I questioned, as I wiped my mouth.

"Hell yea, let me go over to the bar and pay this bill though," he said. Then he got up and headed over to the bar to handle the bill. "Alright Dre we're all good. Now lets hit the lobby, so we can check out and get this shuttle to the airport."

Then we both grabbed our luggage and headed towards the lobby. Ace turned in our keys as he approached the front desk.

"Alright Dre the shuttle will be here in a few so let's just wait outside," he stated as he came back from the front desk.

"Cool, say no more," I said.

Then we grabbed our luggage and headed outside. A few minutes later and the shuttle finally pulled up. The driver politely greeted us as he hopped out. While he helped us with our luggage, we all hopped back in and peeled off to the El Dorado International airport. Forty minutes later and we pulled up at the airport. The driver popped the trunk hopped and helped us with our luggage. I took out my all-black Louis Vuitton wallet and tipped him a fifty to send him about his way. Ace and I then made our way inside the airport and got our luggage checked in. We headed down the terminal and finally copped a squat in the waiting section of our flight.

     "Yo Dre, do you have any of those edibles on you?" he questioned.

     "Yeah, I got you my nigga," I said.

     Then I took out half of a brownie, gave it to Ace and then I ate the other half. A few minutes later and our flight was being called to board. We snatched up our carry on luggage and boarded the plane. Ace didn't waste any time as he put his carry on luggage up, fell into his seat and fell asleep before the plane could even take off. As the plane took off I closed my eyes and proceeded to fall asleep.

     "Dre," Ace said as I started to open my eyes. "We're here."

     We both stood up, grabbed our carry on luggage and made our way out of the plane.

     "Alright Dre, it's been real my nigga but I have to catch my flight back to the Bahamas," he stated.

     "Alright I'll catch you when I catch you," I said.

     We dapped up and went to our waiting sections to catch our flights back home. Unfortunately for me I had a two hour layover, so I just kicked it in the waiting section until my flight was called. Two hours later and my flight was being called. I hopped up, snatched up my carry on luggage and boarded my flight. I put up my carry on luggage as I boarded the plane. I then popped a half of brownie and fell straight to sleep once the plane took off.

     "Damn," I grumpily said as I was forced to endure the rough landing of the plane waking me up.

     The pilot came over the intercom and instructed us to unbuckle our seat belts and exit the plane. Doing as he said, I proceeded down the terminal, all the way to baggage claim and snatched up the rest of my luggage. I headed out the airport and onto the car drop off section. Finding my baby, I popped the trunk and threw my luggage in. Then I hopped in, plugged up my aux cord and blasted Asian Doll's freestyle to Kodak Black's "No Flocking." Then I pulled out the airport and sped off.

I was mad hungry, so I stopped at my favorite chicken spot and picked up spicy chicken wings. A few minutes later and I was pulling into my garage. I snatched up my luggage and spicy chicken, then headed inside through living room up the stairs and onto my room. Since I was leaving tomorrow afternoon, I headed in my closet to repack my luggage. After I repacked my luggage I then grabbed a strawberry swisher and two grams of "Deep Sleep." It was a very potent indica strain that was about to have me knocked the fuck out. I grabbed my spicy chicken and headed downstairs to my living room.

What do I want to watch, I thought to myself. I then sat my food and bud down, on my black and gold marble coffee table. Then I sank down onto my fine leather couch.

"It's Friday, oh hell yeah," I said to myself, as I just remembered one of my newest favorite podcast "Drink Champs" starring one Hip-Hop's finest, Nore, would have a new episode. I turned on the TV, went to my YouTube app and played theie second episode with Ja Rule and Jadakiss.

"Man these niggas are funny as fuck," I thought to myself while dying laughing as I was stuffing the strawberry swisher with some good night time bud.

"Yeah, this is a prefect blunt," I thought to myself as I lit up my blunt and started fucking up my spicy chicken.

The more hard hits I kept taking, the more sleepier I got. So after I finished my food I turned off the T.V, set my alarm, put out my blunt and fell straight to sleep on my couch. I opened my eyes the next morning ,as my alarm sounds off sending Kayne West's song "Ultralight Beam" jamming all throughout my living room. Automatically I hop up off the couch and head upstairs to shower up. *Damn, what am I going to wear?* I thought to myself as I walked into my closet.

It's chilly in New York, so I grabbed my olive colored Glo Gang bomber, black YSL jeans, black Yeezy 950 boots, black Versace belt with the gold medusa buckle and my gold Rolex.

After picking out my fit, I headed into my bathroom and started up my shower.

Twenty minutes later and hopped out to get dressed. I snatched up my luggage, headed downstairs pass my living room and out to my garage. I threw my luggage in the trunk and hopped in. Then I plugged up my aux cord, dropped my top and pulled out the garage.I then blasted YG and Nipsey Hustle's song "Fuck Donald Trump" as I sped off to my warehouse.

"Let me call this nigga now," I said to myself as I was almost at my warehouse. "Yo, what's good, meet me in front of the spot," I instructed as my top grower answered the phone.

"Alright I got you," he said before we hung up. Five minutes later, and I pulled up to my top grower out front waiting on me.

"Yo what's good Dre?" my top grower questioned.

"Shit, nothin' major," I said, as I handed him both bags that had the Costa Rican and Colombian seeds in them. "How's everything here?"

"Everything as been good here, we're getting back to a hundred and ten percent," he said.

"Alright that's what I'm talking about," I happily said.

"Dre, you already know how we do," he said.

"Facts, but I'm about to head up outta here," I stated. "I'll be back in a couple of days."

"Alright bet," he said.

Then I peeled off, outta my warehouse and onto the airport. Twenty five minutes later and I pulled up to the car drop section. I popped the trunk, hopped out and snatched up all my luggage before I headed inside the airport. Once I got inside the airport, I headed over to get my luggage checked in. Then I made my way up the terminal to catch my flight.

"Just in time," I said to myself, as people were already boarding the plane.

I then made my way on the plane and sat in my first class seat. Then I took out a half of a weed brownie ate, relaxed and awaited to touch down in New York City.

CHAPTER VIII

"Excuse me, sir," the flight attendant said as I began to open my eyes. "The plane has just landed."

"Finally," I said to myself.

Then I got up, stretched, and grabbed my carry-on luggage. I then made my way off the plane, down the terminal and onto baggage claim. After I snatched up the rest of my luggage, I made my way out of Laguardia Airport to wait on my limo. Not too much into waiting and the limo pulled up right on side of me. The driver hopped out and helped me with my luggage. Then we both hopped back in and headed off to the Four Seasons hotel in Manhattan.

Man I love coming to New York. I could see the New York City skyline lighting up. A few minutes later and we finally pulled up the hotel. The driver hopped out and helped me with my luggage. Then I tipped him a fifty and sent him on his way.

Damn this building is amazing. I took a moment to feel the up-beat New York vibe. I then headed into the creme marble lobby of the hotel. Then I checked into the "Terrace Park View" executive suite. After checking in, I made my way to the elevator and rode it to my level. Then I hopped off and made my way down the hall to my suite. I entered into my suite and went to the main bedroom and throw my luggage on the bed.

"I need a drink," I said to myself as I raided the refrigerator in search of some good wine. "Oh shit," I said in excitement as I found a bottle of Dusko Blu. "Let me call this plug."

"Yo, my nigga," I said as my plug answered the phone.

"What's good Dre?" he questioned.

"I'm in the city at the Four Seasons and you already know what I need," I stated as I sipped my fine wine.

"I got you," he stated. "Give me fifteen and I'm going to come through with that variety pack."

"Variety pack, that's how you rockin'?" I happily questioned.

"Dre, now you know I'm that nigga out here,"
stated. "You're in NY now, so I'll hook you up with some fronto
and raw rolling papers, on the house."

"Say no more," I said.

"Facts" he said before we both hung up.

"Now let me hit this woman up," I said to myself as I
dialed up Alicia's number.

"DRE!" she happily shouted into the phone as she
answered.

"Damn, I didn't know you missed me that much," I stated
with a chuckle.

"Yeah I missed you, somewhat" she replied with a sweet
tone.

"Where do you want me to meet you at?" I questioned.

"Meet me at Amy Ruth's, 116th Street in Harlem," she
said.

"Alright, I'll see you in thirty," I stated.

"Alright, see you then," she said before we both hung up.
Five minutes later and I started to hear a knock at my door.

"Finally," I said to myself as I looked through the peep hole
and saw that it was my plug.

"You got that for me?" I questioned as I opened the door.

"Yeah, that special," he said as he handed me a
McDonald's bag that smelled like some great bud.

"Damn this is that variety pack," I said as I smelled the bag
more.

"I told you my nigga," he stated as I took out my wallet and
slid him a hundred. "Alright Dre," he said as we dapped hands and
went about our separate ways.

"Alright let me get this Uber," I said to myself.

Then I closed the door, headed to the bedroom and tossed
the McDonald's bag on the bed. I then took out my phone went to
my Uber app and requested a ride.

"It's about to go down tonight," I said to myself.

I made my way out of my suite and down the hall. I hopped
onto the elevator and proceeded to ride it down to the lobby. Then
I headed out the hotel. Immediately I saw my Uber waiting for me
outside. So I hopped in and my Uber pulled off and onto Amy
Ruth's in Harlem. Twenty minutes later and we pulled up to Amy

Ruth's restaurant in Harlem. I took out my wallet and tipped the Uber driver a twenty, as politely thanked him then hopped out.

This is nice and real low-key, I thought to myself as I entered into the restaurant.

Automatically I saw Alicia's light-skin, big booty, fine ass sitting in the corner table by the widow. She looked up at me, smiled and waved me over. I made my way over to her table and coped a squat.

"What's good with you baby girl?" I flirtatious questioned.

"Nothing major, just been working, you know, the usual," she replied as a waiter approached our table.

After taking a short look at the menu that was given to me by the waiter. I decided to order The Reggie Harris, which was southern honey dip fried chicken. The waiter said he would be back momentarily with our food, so we just got back to talking and laughing.

"You'r so funny, Alicia," I said with a laugh.

"Something like that," she playfully said. "Dre, I have to tell you something," she said as she all of sudden switched to a more serious tone.

"Wassup, is everything alright?" I seriously questioned.

"Dre," she said, as tears began to run down her face. "I'm pregnant," she said, with more tears rolling down her face.

"PREGNANT, WHAT THE FUCK?!" I shouted.

I then wiped my face, stood up and walked out as everyone was looking at us. "What the fuck," I angrily said to myself as I walked down the block and requested an Uber from the app. Fifteen minutes later and the Uber pulled up to the curb. I hopped in and told the Uber to drop me off at the Four Seasons.

Twenty minutes later and we pulled up to the hotel. I automatically hopped out and made my way in the lobby. I headed to the elevator, rode it up to my level and hopped out, before then heading down the hall and into my suite.

I need some bud for this bullshit. I then went into the master bedroom and snatched up the McDonald's bag. Then I headed out to the terrace, that overlooked Central Park and started rolling up. Since I walked out before the food came at the restaurant, I was mad hungry, so I called up the hotel and ordered a mushroom cheese pizza and spicy chicken wings.

"Shit I need to call Niniette, this shit is crazy," I said to myself as I dialed her up. "I fucked up, Niniette," I said before she could even speak into the phone.

"What are you talking about Dre?" she questioned.

"Man I really fucked up" I stated as I hit my joint.

"Dre if you don't stop repeating yourself and tell me what the fuck your talking about," she sternly questioned.

"O.K, I went to have dinner with this woman I met on my trip to Nicaragua with John last month," I stated. "So she breaks out in tears as she was telling me that she's pregnant."

"PREGNANT!" she shouted into the phone.

"Yeah pregnant," I said with a sigh.

"Well how did you react Dre?" she questioned.

"Sorta like you just did," I replied.

"What did she say?" she questioned.

"I don't know, I got up and left as soon as she said it," I said.

"Damn Dre, what the fuck is wrong with you?" she angrily questioned.

"Niniette I wasn't trying to hear that shit," I sternly replied.

"Fuck what you were trying to hear Dre" she stated. "You should of stayed and comforted her, lord knows she's really going through it."

"Fuck, you're right, Niniette," I said with a sigh.

"You need to hit her up and talk to her Dre," she said.

"Alright Niniette, I'll hit her up," I said.

"You need to," she stated as I started to hear a knock at the door.

"I got you, but I'll hit you up later," I said.

"Alright Dre, later," she said.

"Later," I said before we both hung up.

I then got up and headed to the door. "Yes, finally my food," I said, as I looked through the peep hole and saw that it was a man carrying food. I then opened the door and grabbed my food. Then I walked over to the living room of the suite and sat my food on coffee table. I went back in the bedroom to get my chromecast flash drive out my luggage. I plugged up my chromecast flash drive to the T.V, went to my YouTube app, and played Tax Stone's new episode off "Tax Season." I rolled up some more bud to light up and ate my food while listening to this funny ass nigga Tax talking that real shit with Philly's top goon, AR-AB.

Shit was still raining heavy on my head after I finished my food and blunt, so I grabbed the bottle of D'usse I saw in the refrigerator, then headed to the bathroom and ran a nice, warm soaking bath. I headed back into the bedroom to snatch up my Beats Pill. Then I walked back over to the living room, rolled up another joint and headed to the bathroom. I sat my Beats Pill on the marble counter top and blasted Kayne West's song "Ultralight Beam." Then I lit my joint, poured me up a shot of D'usse and hopped into the deep soaking tub. Man I was feelin' to right off the bud and D'usse. But at the same time I was still trying to accept the fact that I got shorty pregnant.

"What the fuck am I going to do?" I questioned myself as I downed another shot of D'usse.

Niniette is right though, if I was man enough to cum inside of her, then I should be man enough to take care of what comes out. Maybe this a sign, letting me know it's about that time to change my ways and find someone to keep me grounded. Fuck I'm tired.

I hopped out the tub, dried off and headed into the bedroom. I then passed out on the king size bed. The next morning I woke up with a slight hangover, but I still had to get it together and dial up Alicia.

"What do you want Dre?" Alicia questioned before I could say anything.

"Alicia, I apologize for how I acted last night," I stated. "Can we please meet up for breakfast or something?"

"I don't know Dre," she replied.

"Please Alicia, please!" I seriously pleaded.

"Alright fine, Dre where do you want to meet up at?" she questioned.

"Meet me at The Garden, it's a restaurant in the Four Seasons," I said.

"Alright, I'll text you when I'm there," she said before she hung up.

After wrapping up my convo with Alicia I went in my luggage and laid out my fit. I felt like dressing up so I laid out my

107

white H&M button down, black Zara khakis, black Zara blazer and my all-velvet black Ralph Lauren loafers. Then I headed to the bathroom started up a warm shower and hopped in. Fifteen minutes later I hopped out, headed into the bedroom and got dressed.

"Let me smoke one before I go meet up with shorty," I said to myself.

I headed into the living room and rolled up some of that good variety pack. I blazed up and relaxed as I waited for Alicia to text me. Five minutes later and I get a text from Alicia saying she just made it to the hotel. So I put out my blunt, made my way out the suite and down the hall.

As I walked into the restaurant I saw Alicia sitting at one of the tables by nicely decorated red flowers. I made my way over to the table and immediately started apologizing.

"Dre you don't have to keep apologizing, I understand your emotions and I genuinely forgive you," she stated as a waiter came over to take our order.

I wasn't to hungry so I just ordered a cinnamon raisin bagel, whole wheat omelet wrap and a glass of freshly squeezed orange juice.

"So what the fuck are we going to do Alicia?" I questioned as the waiter left.

"Religiously I don't believe in abortions, so that's out the window," she said.

"I understand and respect that," I stated. "But how is this going to work with me in Seattle and you in New York?" I questioned, as the waiter came back with our drinks then eventually our food.

"With your lifestyle, it's better I have full custody until you're more stable," she replied as we both started eating.

"Alicia, I don't know how I feel about full custody though," I stated.

"Dre how many days have you been home before you came here?" she questioned.

"Shit like one," I said as I started to see her point.

"Exactly, I don't want to keep you away from our child but your schedule is too hectic," she stated as we finished up our breakfast.

"Yeah, you're right," I stated. "I have to make a few more moves anyway, before I can be less hands on with my work."

"Alright Dre and I'm not going to put you on child support or anything," she stated.

"That's cool, but I was already planning on sending you money anyway," I said.

"Alright Dre, I really appreciate that," she stated.

"I'll be contacting you to let you know how I'm doing," she said as she got up.

"Let me walk you out," I said. Then I got up and we made our way out the restaurant, pass the lobby and out of the hotel.

"Alright Dre, that's my Uber," she said as looked at me with tears in her eyes.

"Alicia come here, it's going to be O.K," I said. Then I grabbed her by her hand, hugged her tight and kissed her on the forehead.

"I really appreciate you, Dre," she said as she looked up at me.

"No problem, now go catch your Uber before he leaves," I said as I let her go.

"I'll call you later, Dre," she said as she hopped in the Uber and left.

"Damn this shit is stressful," I said to myself as I headed down the block.

In my drunken state the night before, I came to the conclusion that I need to go ahead and lock something down. So I made my way over the the 47th St. of Manhattan, otherwise known as the Diamond District. A few blocks later and I approached the Diamond District.I head into a few shops. The first two shops, I saw some some dope rings but nothing that was too amazing. I searched high and low for that special piece, but I just couldn't find it. Not even the third and fourth shops I went to had it. By that time I was ready to give up. But not until I headed over to the fifth store and fell in love with this beautiful, quarter of a million dollar ring. The ring have a beautiful large VVS cut Amethyst gemstone surrounded by a bunch of VVS cut diamonds.
The Amethyst gemstone ring is what I was looking for this whole time. It symbolized spiritual energy and enlightenment.
Whoever I prepose to is going to die in joy when they see

109

this ring, I thought to myself as I made my way out the store.

I made my way down a few blocks and headed towards my hotel. Damn I came to hit something and fucked around and got hit with something. But I'm not trippin' anymore, a nigga is about to be a father out here in these streets.

A couple of blocks later and I then approached the hotel. I made my way through the lobby and to the elevator. I hopped on that joint, rode it up to my level and hopped off. I then made my way down the hall and into my suite. Immediately, I headed into the bedroom and packed up my luggage.

So much for gettin' some good-good on this trip.

Then I made my way out the suite, down the hall and onto the elevator. I checked in my room key and headed outside to wait for my limo.

"Damn so much is going on in my life I think I need a major vacation," I said to myself as I saw the limo turning the corner.

The limo pulled up on the curb and the the driver hopped out and politely greeted me. He helped me get my luggage in the trunk, we both hopped back in and he took off to Laguardia airport. Low-key I was kind of sad to leave New York. New York is just a hustler's dream. I really wish weed was legal out here. Lords knows I would be out here with three or four shops in every borough.

Forty minutes later and we finally pulled up to the airport. The driver hopped out and helped me get my luggage out the trunk. I politely thanked him and tipped him a fifty, to send him about his way. I then made my way inside the airport and checked-in my luggage. Then I headed up the terminal and waited at the gate of my flight. Just as I was about to really kick back and get comfortable, my flight was being called.

Time to head back home.

I snatched up my carry on luggage and made my way to board the plane. Making my way onto the plane I just remembered I lost the other half of my weed brownie. But I was already mad tired, so I just passed out as soon as the plane took off.

"Damn what the fuck," I said to myself as the roughness of the plane landing woke me up.

A few minutes later and the pilot came over the intercom

and instructed us to unbuckle our seat belts and exit the plane. I then hopped up outta' my seat and snatched up my carry-on luggage. Finally, I headed out the airport and made my way to the car drop off section.

"Fuck, now I have to tell shorty that I'm about to have a kid," I said to myself.

I threw my luggage in the back seat and sped off to my crib. Twenty minutes later and I finally made it back home after a short stressful trip. I snatched up my luggage and headed inside past the living room, up the stairs, and into my bedroom.

"Let me hit up shorty real quick," I said to myself as I tossed my luggage in my closest and dialed her up.

"DRE I'M SO HAPPY TO HEAR FROM YOU!" Christine said with excitement, before I could even say anything.

"Well damn, you act like you haven't seen me in forever," I playfully stated.

"I know, but it sure does feel like it," she said.

"Well in that case, do you want to go to dinner tonight?" I questioned.

"I would love to, Dre" she replied. "I just can't spend the night, I have a big test in the morning."

"Alright that's cool, just meet at the Hidden Habor at eight o' clock," I stated.

"Alright Dre, see you then," she said before we both hung up.

I wanted to be stupid fresh, so I walked over to my closet and snatched up my black Ralph Lauren Purple Label cashmere sweater, black crocodile Louis belt, black Zara slacks and black Hermes loafers. Then headed into my bathroom, started up a nice warm shower and hopped in.

Fifteen minutes later and I hopped out and got dressed. I headed downstairs, past the living room and into my garage. Then I started up the whip and pulled off to "Hidden Habor Yachts."

"Damn, how am I going to tell shorty I got another chick pregnant?" I asked myself as I approached the parking lot of Hidden Harbor Yachts.

I parked my whip, hopped out and saw Christine standing by the docks.

"You look so fine, beloved," I said, as I grabbed her waist

111

from behind and gave her a kiss on the lips.

"I've really been missing you Dre," she stated as I let her go, took her hand and lead her down the dock.

"This is a really nice boat," she stated as we approached the boat.

"I know, I wish it was mine," I replied. "One of my best clients, lets me use from time to time."

The boat was pretty dope, it was all white with thick black stripes on the sides. The light of the full moon lit up the Seattle sky, so I decided to have dinner on the top deck.

"Dre, this is beautiful," she stated.

Then we sat down and I took off the tops of the Italian style dinner, I had one of the chefs whip up and deliver. I poured us up a glass of Dom Perignon, as we began eating, talking and just overall enjoying each others company. As we finished up our dinner I was really starting to down the champagne. I needed to muster up enough liquid courage to tell her about the pregnancy.

"Christine I have to tell you some real shit," I said in a serious tone as I downed my glass of fine champagne.

"What is it Dre?" she questioned with a concern tone.

"A couple of months ago I met a woman on one of my trips," I poured up some more champagne.

"Ok, so what the fuck are you trying to tell me Dre?" she said as I could tell she was about to lose her shit.

"Long story short, we had sex and now she's pregnant," I said.

Then I downed my glass and prepared for the worst. The whole thirty seconds she spent looking at me in disgust felt like an eternity.

"Don't ever contact me again in your life!" she angrily stated. She then grabbed her glass, stood up and looked me dead in my eyes. She threw the champagne all over my face and left me sitting all by my tipsy, lonely self.

Since I was feeling a little something off the Dom Perignon, I decided to chill out for a bit before I headed home. Twenty minutes later and I start to sober up. So I made my way off the boat, down the dock and to the parking lot. Then I hopped in my whip and peeled off back to my spot.

"Man I have to call Niniette, this shit is to much," I said to myself as I pulled into my garage.

"What's up Dre?" Niniette questioned as she answered the phone.

"Shit nothin' major, I just came from seeing that college girl I was telling you about," I said. Then I hopped out the car and headed inside.

"Oh really and how did that go?" she curiously questioned.

"Not well, I met up with her to tell her about the pregnancy," I said as made it up the stairs and into my room.

"Oh shit now this I got to hear," she said with a laugh.

"I'm glad you think this is funny," I stated. "Shorty straight threw some good Dom Perignon all up in yo' boy's face." I said, as I kicked off my shoes and jumped on my comfortable California king size bed.

"Damn it went down like that Dre?" she said.

"Hell yeah, I told her to meet me for dinner at Hidden Habor," I stated. "I had a nice little Italian dinner set up and shit, then we got to kicking it as usual. I tried to soften her up with the Dom Perignon before I told her but that didn't work."

"Well at least you went out on a fancy bang," she said.

"I know but it's still fucked up, I really liked her," I said as I decided which night time strain I felt like smoking.

"Dre you can't have your cake and eat it too," she stated.

"I know, but I'm going to hit you up later I'm about to roll up," I said. I grabbed two grams of the indica strain God's Bud and a wine Dutch master.

"Alright Dre, later," she said before we both hung up.

The wind was pretty still chill tonight, so I decided to go out to the balcony and smoke. The last seventy-two hours have been so mother fuckin' hectic. *It's just good to relax with a nice blunt,* I thought to myself while taking deep hits. After I finished my blunt I headed back inside, jumped straight on my comfortable king size bed, and fell straight to sleep.

CHAPTER IX

The next morning I woke up at day break.

"Fuck," I said to myself with a sigh of relief as I stretched my long body. I hopped out off the bed and into my closet to grab some good morning medicine.

"What strain do I want to smoke?" I questioned to myself as I looked through my jars of sativa. "Oh shit I haven't smoked this in a minute," I said to myself as I grabbed two grams of Amnesia Haze.

Then I grabbed a backwood and headed downstairs to cook up some breakfast. I decided to eat something sweet, so I sat my bud and backwood to the side. Then I went in my fridge and grabbed a couple of eggs and some cannbutter. This french toast is going to be sweet as hell. I grabbed some cinnamon, brown sugar and thin sliced French bread out my pantry. Before I got to cooking, I rolled up my fat ass backwood and turned on the kitchen T.V to some soccer. I took my non-stick skillet out, sat it on the stove and turned the heat up half way. Then I took a few tablespoons of cannbutter and let it melt in the skillet. I dipped my thin slice, French bread in the egg yolk and showered it with cinnamon and brown sugar. I then tossed it on the skillet and cooked both sides until they were golden brown. I didn't really feel like eating out on my terrace or in the living room, so I just ate in the kitchen, plus this MLS soccer match was getting pretty good.

After pouring me up some good lemonade I finally lit my fat ass backwood. I proceeded to eat my cannabis infused thin slice French toast French bread.

"Oh shit," I said to myself as I just realized I needed to get up with John to fill him in on this crazy ass shit.

"Yo, what's good with you Dre?" John questioned as he answered the phone.

"Shit you know I been hustlin', but yo my nigga are busy today?" I questioned. "I need to get up with you."

"Shit, the only thing I had going on is a paintball game," he stated. "Are you trying to ride?"

"Nigga hell yea, when and where?" I happily said as I finished up my breakfast and kept smokin' off this find herb.

"It's at Northwest Paintball Park Inc. in three hours, but I'm going to come scoop you up so be ready in an hour," he said.

"Alright my nigga," I said before we both hung up. Paintball shooting? This should be fun.

Finishing my backwood, I hopped up, washed my dishes and headed upstairs to get ready.

"What should I wear?" I questioned myself as I searched through my closet. "Yup this is perfect." I grabbed an all black nike hoodie, black nike sweatpants and all-black nike Hustle Heart sneakers. I laid out my fit on my bed and headed into my bathroom to shower up.

Twenty minutes later and I hop out the shower, get dressed and roll me up another backwood. I smoked on my balcony while I waited for John to text me. Another twenty minutes went by I finally got a text from John telling me he's out front. So I made my way downstairs and out my front door to John parked up on the curb.

"What's good my nigga?" John questioned as we dapped up.

"Shit nothin', just ready to twist these mark ass niggas' caps back," I said as I hopped in his whip.

"Shit say no more, we out," he stated. He pulled off the curb and onto Northwest Paintball Park. An hour later we pull up to Northwest Paintball Park Inc.

"Damn it's mad people here," I said as I looked around the parking lot.

"Yeah it is, majority of these people are playing in the match we're playing in," he said.

"So how is this about to work?" I questioned.

"Basically it's teams of two's, three's and four's starting off on the Fort Sasquatch Field. Then we'll be moving to the woods for round two."

John then popped the trunk as we hopped out and got suited up.

"Oh shit John this is how we rockin'?" I asked as John loaded up a mock model AK-47 paintball gun.

"Dre, now you know I only fuck with big toys," he said as he loaded up the mock model M16 and glocks. "Alright Dre, are you ready?" he questioned, as we stuck both glock paintball guns in our holsters.

"Hell yeah, let's do this shit," I replied.

Then we headed over to the battlefield. Man this was a real serious ass game of paintball. There were at least twenty teams on the Fort Sasquatch Field.

"IS EVERYONE READY?" an announcer said with a bullhorn.

"YES!" everyone yelled.

The announcer blew his horn and everyone took off to their hideouts while blasting their competition.

"DRE, LETS GO," John shouted as we took the fuck off towards a big dune buggy.

Shit was definitely lit, I was bustin' the fuck out of niggas left and right. Then John and I finally made it over to the big ass dune buggy.

"Dre hop in the second seat and bust these fuck niggas, I'm going to drive around field," he said.

I strapped up in the high rise second seat and John strapped up in the low rise driver seat.

"DRE LOOK ALIVE, WE AT THESE MARK ASS NIGGAS' HEADS!!" he shouted with excitement as he punched

116

that bitch, running dials up on the dash.

"THIS SHIT IS LIT" I shouted as I saw a gang of niggas letting their bitches rip off dirt bikes and ATV's. "Yo this is like some wild ass GTA and Call Of Duty shit."

We make two more laps around then John drives off into a cut.

"YOU GOOD?" John shouted, as he cut off the engine.

"YEAH I'M STRAIGHT, BUT HELP A NIGGA OUT WITH THESE CONFUSING ASS BUCKLES!" I shouted.

John unbuckled himself and then helped me get out my seat.

"Yo what's move?" I questioned .

"We're about to take those two dirt bikes over there and ride off into the woods," he replied. "The horn is about to sound off any second now, which means it's round two. So everyone is about to head off into the woods.

Soon as we heard the horn, we rushed over to the bikes. Then we hopped on, started them up and sped off into the woods.

"FOLLOW ME BRU!" John shouted, as he sped up in front of me.

Finally John slows down and makes a stop by mad bushes.

"Alright Dre, we're about to stash the bikes in the bushes, then climb this tree that has a balcony hideout," he said.

We stashed the bikes in the bushes and proceeded to head to the tree top hideout. Luckily the tree top hideout had make-shift wooden steps craved in, I didn't know shit about free climbing trees.

"Shit, we're re high as fuck," I said as I looked down from the tree top hideout.

"Naw my nigga, we're not high as fuck yet," he stated. Then he pulled out a fat ass blunt he had stuffed in his clothing.

"My nigga, that's what I'm talkin' about," I said as John lit up the blunt and passed it to me. After we finished smoking we checked our straps to make sure everything was straight.

"Yo John, you hear that shit?" I said as I started to hear branches cracking.

"Dre, if you don't pipe your paranoid ass down" he replied. "There is a reason why we're up here, you can see everything."

"Shit, maybe you're right but keep your trigger finger live,"

I said as I reloaded my clip.

"Dre you don't have to tell me twice," he said.

Right after he said that we started hearing POP-POP-POP.

"OH SHIT, I TOLD YOU NIGGA!" I shouted as I started shooting ground level.

"WHAT THE FUCK, THESE NIGGAS ARE EVERYWHERE," John said.

Then I looked around and noticed mad niggas in the surrounding trees, blastin' at our shit.

"JOHN, I DON'T KNOW HOW LONG WE CAN KEEP THIS UP!" I shouted.

"NIGGA, WE'RE NOT GOIN' OUT LIKE NO HOES," he shouted. "WE'RE EXCHANGING PAINT UNTIL OUR HAMMERS CLICK."

After five minutes of an intense paintball shoot, we both were out of ammunition and had to wave our white flags. Niggas were cheering like fuck after our defeat, since we were the strongest team on the battlefield.

"Come on Dre, let's dip up outta' here," John said.

We climbed down from the tree and scooped up our bikes from where we stashed them. We hopped on and sped off, all the way back to the parking lot. We left the bikes in the parking lot, John pops his trunk and we tossed the straps and paintball gear in and hopped in.

"Yo Dre, weren't you suppose to get up with me about something?" he questioned Then he took out a wine Dutch master and some mango smelling bud to roll up.

"Oh yeah I was, so you remember that woman I met when we were in Nicaragua?" I questioned.

"Hell yeah? I remember those two freaks," he said as he lit up the blunt.

"Well I went to New York to see her," I said as John passed me the blunt.

"Oh shit, so how did it go down?" he questioned.

"My nigga," I said as I let out some smoke, then passed him the blunt. "Shorty told me she's pregnant."

"WHAT?" he shouted as he choked on his smoke.

"Yup," I said with a sigh.

"Dre, my nigga, please don't tell me you believe that shit," he said as he passed me the blunt.

"My nigga I don't know if she's lying or telling the truth, but until I know for facts I have to be there for shorty," I said before hitting the blunt.

"You're right my nigga, but Dre you have to be careful out here," he said.

"I know my nigga this shit got me low-key stressin', I need a mother fuckin' vacation," I said as I passed him the blunt.

"Speaking of a vacation, my nigga I found this dope ass spa island resort," he said.

"Word, where at my nigga?" I questioned in excitement as he passed me the blunt.

"South Africa," he said.

"The motherland, my nigga? Oh shit, it's lit," I happily said.

"Hell yeah, I'll text you the info later," he said.

"Alright my nigga, good lookin'," I said.

After we finished up the blunt, John pulled off to drop me off back at my spot. As we we're cruisin' I started to put a lot of thought into different things, going on in my life. But after John started telling me about this vacation spot, I started to look at things a little bit brighter. An hour later and we were pulling up to my crib.

"Alright Dre, I'll text you the details about the trip later," John stated.

"Alright my nigga good lookin'," I said as we dapped up.

I hopped out his whip and made my way to the front door of my crib and headed in. Immediately I headed upstairs and changed into some old Adidas sweats. Then I headed into my closet, to grab 3.5 grams of some "Bubba Kush" and a pre-cloned, raw rolling paper. I was mad hungry after all that paint balling, so I snatched up my bud and pre-cloned raw, and then headed downstairs to my kitchen.

"Shit what should I cook up?" I questioned to myself as I ran-sacked my fridge. "Yes bruh," I said to myself in the excitement as I found some more crab legs in my fridge.

I grabbed my big ass pot and filled it up with water. I seasoned it with some salt, pepper and lemon pepper, and threw in the crab legs.

After I tossed in my crabs legs I took a seat by the TV and turned it on. "Oh shit TSU Surf & Tay Roc versus DNA & K-Shine!" I said, as checked the new rap battles on YouTube. I know this battle was going to be raw!

After the wild ass battle that TSU Surf & Tay Roc obviously won, I walked over to my stove, cut it off, and plated my crab. I poured me up a half glass of D'usse and headed into my living room to eat. I finally got the text from John about the vacation spot in South Africa, as I sat down and started eating.

"Oh shit this is lit," I said as I checked out the website of the vacation spot. I automatically knew who I wanted to take on the trip, so I dialed up Niniette.

"Wassup Dre?" Niniette questioned as she answered the phone.

"Nothin' major but what do you got on your schedule for the week after next?" I questioned as I took a sip of the fine D'usse.

"Nothing really," she replied.

"Alright pack your bags then, in two weeks we're going to this spa island resort in South Africa," I said.

"Damn for real Dre?" she questioned in excitement.

"Yes Niniette I got you, I'll send you the details a little bit later," I replied.

"Alright Dre," she stated.

"Alright then Niniette I'll catch up with you later," I said.

"Alright then and thanks Daddy," she said in her little kid voice that she always uses when I get her something or take her somewhere.

"Whatever, later baby girl," I said with a chuckle before we both hung up.

After I got off the phone with Niniette I slowly finished up my crab legs, while also feeling that D'usse creeping up on a nigga. I just kicked back on my couch for a few in a real drunken haze.

Eventually I hopped up, headed upstairs and checked into bed since I did have to check up on things at the warehouse the following day. My alarm clock that I set for noon the next day went off, sending Drake's "Tuscan Leather" melodically blasting all throughout my room. I automatically hop up, head to my bathroom and start up a warm ass shower then I hopped in. Fifteen minutes later, I hop out and walk over to my closet. I threw on my white and black adidas tracksuit and white and black adidas sneaks to match. I then headed downstairs to my kitchen to blend me up a strawberry, kiwi and kale smoothie. After I blended me up a nice sweet and healthy smoothie, I headed past my living room and into my garage.Then I hopped in my whip, started it up and pulled out then sped off to my warehouse.Twenty minutes later and I pull up to my warehouse.

"Hopefully everything is everything, I don't need any bullshit before I head off to my trip," I said to myself as I hopped out and made my way inside.

"What's good with you Dre?" my top grower questioned as I entered inside.

"Shit, nothin' major I just came to check up on everything," I replied.

"Well everything is straight, but let me show you how everything is growing," he stated. We made our way inside to check out my plants. "Alright Dre, so these are the clones of that Jamaican shit you had," he said as I examined the plant.

"Damn, this shit smells wonderful!" I expressed.

"I know and it's growing faster and bigger than we expected," he said.

"How is that new shit I brought from Costa Rica and Colombia doing?" I questioned.

"It's still in the vegetation state, but Dre the guys and I came up with an amazing idea," he said with excitement.

"What is it?" I questioned.

"I think we should cross breed the Jamaican, Costa Rican and Colombian planets," he said.

"OH SHIT!" I shouted.

"That would be an amazing idea, hell yeah do that shit," I said.

"I knew you were going to fuck with it, but alright Dre we got you," he stated.

"Alright cool good lookin' " I said."I'm about to head up outta here, I'll catch up with you later."

"Alright Dre," he said.

"Oh yeah and in two weeks I'm going to be on vacation for a good little minute, so I need you niggas to hold shit down," I said. "I don't need any bullshit."

"Dre do you really even have to say that, you know how we rock," he replied.

"Shit you're right, that's a fact, but alright though bruh, I'll catch you later," I said as we dapped up.

Then I made my way out, hopped in my whip and took off.

A week later and I peacefully awoke on the morning of my departure to South Africa. I immediately hopped out of bed and headed over to my bathroom. I started up a warm shower and hopped in. Fifteen minutes later and I hopped out the shower. I headed over to my closet and threw on my all-black & gold striped OVO sweatsuit and my all-black OVO Jordan 10 sneaks. I snatched up my luggage and headed downstairs. Then I sat my luggage by the garage door and headed into my kitchen.

Since we were going to be a on a twenty hour flight, I decided to make us some cannabis infused strawberry and pineapple smoothies. I tossed my regular ingredients into the blender and added some cannabis infused almond milk. After I finish blending up my smoothie, I dialed up Niniette to make sure she was ready.

"Yo, are you ready?" I questioned as soon as she answered the phone.

"Dre don't ask me, like I the one that's always running late and yes I am," she replied.

"Don't be gettin' smart now and alright cool, I'll see you in ten," I stated.

"Alright Dre, see you then," she said before we both hung up.

I poured our smoothies up in some glass cup containers and headed out past my living to my garage door. I snatched up my luggage, headed out the door, popped my trunk and threw my luggage in. I then pulled out of my garage and toward Niniette's crib.

Ten minutes later and I pulled up to Niniette's lakeside townhouse.

"LET'S GO!" I shouted as I honked the horn.

"DRE, SHUT THE FUCK UP!" Niniette shouted back, as I hopped out to help her with her luggage.

"Girl who the fuck are you talking to?" I questioned as I grabbed her by her waist.

"I'm talking to you nigga," she said with a chuckle before I passionately kissed her on the lips.

"Alright baby girl, let's head over to the airport," I stated as I let her go.

Then we hopped in the whip and headed to the airport. Twenty five minutes later and we pulled up to the airport. Since we were taking a private jet that one of my top clients let me use, we had to pull up all the way to the landing and take off strips.

"I didn't know we were flying private, Dre," she stated with excitement.

We then hopped out and snatched up our luggage from the trunk. Then we proceeded onto the plane and coped a squat in the main living section of plane as we waited to take off to Cape Town, South Africa.

CHAPTER X

After the plane took off and cruised very high in the sky, we snatched up our smoothies and headed to the master suite of the plane.

"Dre I didn't know you had breakfast set up for us," Niniette stated as I popped the bottle of Bel Air champagne that was cooling off in a bucket of ice.

"Yeah, I kind of figured you would be hungry," I replied, as I poured us some Bel Air. "Let's toast," I said, as I picked up my glass.

"To what Dre?" she questioned with a chuckle.

"To life, love, and internal peace" I replied. We tapped our glasses and began to eat our breakfast.

"Dre did you bring some bud?" she questioned, as we finished up our breakfast.

"Hell yeah, why? Are you trying to smoke right now?" I questioned.

"Yeah even though these weed smoothies are about to have us passed the fuck out in the next hour, I'm still trying to get faded now," she said.

"Shit I feel you, hold up let me go grab this shit," I stated.

I went out to the main living section of the plane and snatched up my Gucci duffle bag. When I made my way back inside of the master suite, Niniette was already dressed all the way down looking sexy as hell.

"Hurry up and roll Dre," she flirtatiously expressed with a smile.

I took out a couple of sheets of tobacco and proceeded to roll up two Khalifa Kush cigars, one for now and another for when we head to the hotel.

"Yo Niniette we're going to have to use this smoke buddy shit," I said as I started to get undressed.

"What the fuck is a smoke buddy?" she curiously questioned.

"It's this personal filter thing you blow your excess smoke into," I stated. "I normally don't use it, but I'm not trying to hear this pilots mouth." I grabbed my cigar, lighter and smoke buddy and hopped into bed.

"Let me fire this shit up Dre," she said as she snatched the Khalifa Kush cigar out my hands.

"First of all, why you snatchin' my shit, I should snatch yo ass up", I stated. "Second of all, what you know about cigars?" I questioned as I handed her my light.

"Snatch who, nigga please," she said with a chuckle. "And furthermore I'm ten years your senior, so don't act like I haven't been around the block."

She lit up the cigar and hit the fuck out that shit. Man this woman knows how to talk that shit, light my shit and hit my shit. *I swear I'm going to marry this chick,* I thought to myself as I watched her take the Khalifa Kush smoke like a straight G.

After about forty minutes of getting lifted off the Khalifa Kush cigar smoke, Niniette was ready to join the mile high club so you know what popped off next. Three hours later and we both passed the fuck out. The weed smoothies really started to hit us, so I already knew we would be waking up in Cape Town, South Africa. I woke up thirty minutes before we were going to land, so I hopped up out of bed, got dressed and woke up Niniette. After she got dressed we made our way to the main seating section of the plane. The pilot came over the intercom and instructed us to buckle up and prepare to land. As we were touching down I was amazed by how beautiful the night time Cape Town skyline was. The plane landed pretty smooth as we finally landed at Cape Town International Airport.

Niniette and I snatched up our luggage and made our way off the plane and onto the landing strip, where we had an new 2016 Mercedes waiting on us to take us to the resort. We then made our way over to our ride with all of our luggage. As we approached the car, the driver hopped out and helped us with our luggage. Then we all hopped in and pulled off to Only & Only resort. Luckily Cape Town International Airport was only eighteen minutes away from the resort, so we pulled up to the beautifully lit resort that was on it's own island close by the coast of Cape Town. The driver hopped out and helped us with our luggage. I tipped him a fifty to send him on his way.

"Damn Dre, this resort is so amazing," Niniette said as we headed into lobby.

After checking in at the front desk, we made our to the elevator and rode it up to our floor. Soon as we got into the suite, I called up the front desk and requested a chef to come cook up some hot wings, since the suite had a full size kitchen.

"Oh shit it's lit" I said as I peeped the welcome bottle of red wine and fresh fruit platter.

We then walked passed the large dining section that had a nice twelve seat cherrywood table. Then we passed the huge living section and into the very huge master bedroom where we tossed our luggage by the bed.

"DRE, SNATCH UP THAT WINE, SOME GLASSES, FRUIT PLATTER AND CIGAR!" Niniette shouted from the bathroom as I heard her running up a bath.

I headed back out the room, past the living section and to the dining section. I grabbed the bottle of wine, some glasses and the fresh fruit platter and headed back into the master bedroom. I then went in my luggage and snatched up my marijuana filled cigar and headed into the bathroom. I sat the fresh fruit platter, wine glasses and wine bottle to the slide. I handed Niniette the cigar and lighter, then I got undressed and opened up the bottle of wine. I poured our glasses up and slid in the big ass stone tub.

"Dre you always make me feel like a queen when I'm with you, but I wish you wouldn't entertain all these women," she stated as she passed the cigar and sipped her wine.

"Niniette I'm officially done entertaining these women," I replied. "I have a baby on the way; I can't keep acting like a little boy."

I hit the cigar slow and heavy while feeding Niniette some strawberries.

"Well about damn time" she replied. "I wish you would of came to that realization before getting someone pregnant, but fuck it, as least you know now," she said as she feed me a pineapple slice.

We talked, laughed, smoke, drank and overall vibed it out in the warm soaking tub. That was until we heard the front door shut.

"That was probably the chef leaving, so our wings must be done," I said as I put out the marijuana filled cigar.

We hopped out the tub, dried off and put on some bathrobes. We then headed to the kitchen and snatched up our wings.

"Dre, get a bottle of something nice and smooth," she stated.

I raided the bar and found a nice ass bottle of XO D'usse. Since it was pretty warm we decided to eat our wings out on the terrace, which had an amazing view of Table Mountain. After drinking, eating and taking in the breath taking views of Table Mountain, we headed back inside to the master bedroom and fell into a drunken sleep.

The next morning I started to wake up to Niniette kissing and nubbin' on the back of my ear.

"What the fuck are you doing?" I questioned with a chuckle.

"I'm trying to wake your bum ass up," she playfully replied with a smile. "What do you have planned for us today?"

"After we eat breakfast we're heading out to Cape Town wine lands to go taste some good food and wine at Belheim Wine Estate, then we're coming back here for a massage," I stated. "Then after the massage we're going up to Table mountain, so let's go." Then I smacked her on big her ass booty as I hopped out of bed.

I went over to my luggage and snatched up my Beats Pill. I went into the bathroom and sat my Beats Pill on the marble counter. Then I blasted Erykah Badu's album "Baduizm" off my Tidal music app.

"HURRY UP!" I shouted as I started us up a warm shower and hopped in.

"DRE, IF YOU DON'T SHUT THE FUCK UP, RUSHING ME," she shouted back, then finally came and joined me in the shower.

After thirty minutes of washing, rubbing, scrubbing and a little lovin', we hopped out and headed into the room to get dressed.

"Look at you playing stylist for me" I stated, as I noticed Niniette had laid out an white Tommy Hilfiger polo shirt, tan

Gucci slacks, white Stacy Adam loafers and my all gold Rolex watch.

"See while you were over here rushing me, I was playing my position and laying yo' shit out," she playfully stated as she rolled her eyes.

I grabbed her by her waist kissed her on her forehead and told her thank you. We then made our way out the suite and down the hall. Then onto the elevator and rode it down to the lobby. Then we headed over to the restaurant inside the hotel. Once we entered into the restaurant of the hotel, we made our way over to the tables that had views of the hotel's pool.

As we took our seats, a waiter came over and politely greeted us and took our orders. Niniette ordered the Greek salad and I proceeded to order the Garlic Cream Norwegian Salmon. The waiter told us he would be back with our menus shortly, so Niniette and I just chopped it up about the usual shit. Not too much into hearing Niniette's crazy ass talking about her crazy ass and our waiter came back out with our food. A couple of big, mouth watering bites later and we were finishing up our food.

After finishing breakfast we then headed out to the lobby, as I requested and scheduled a shuttle to take us over to Belheim Wine Estate and pick us up. We then made our way out the lobby just as our shuttle was pulling up. The driver hopped out politely greeted us and opened our door. Then we hopped in and pulled off the curb and onto to Belheim Wine Estate. Not even fifteen minutes into our journey, and Niniette already had her big ass head laying on my chest. She was passed out sleep, but I always love it when she does that, it makes me feel like more of a man.

As we were coasting through empty lines, I looked out the window and was just so amazed by where I was. My dream always was to adventure out to the motherland, and now that it's happening, it's just surreal. Damn this shit crazy. Who would of thought, a twenty-five year-old black male, from the crime written and poverty stricken slums of Southside Chicago, would achieve so much. Man if I would of never believed in myself; I would of never reached these heights. It's really true what they say, if you put your mind to something you can achieve it.

Twenty seven minutes later and we pulled up to Belheim Wine Estate.

"Niniette, we're here," I said as I gave her, big wet kisses on the cheek, multiple times to wake her up.

After waking up, we then hopped out and made our way to the entrance of the winery. As we entered, we were politely greeted by the workers. We actually had just made it in time for the wine yard tour. So Niniette and I made our way back outside, and hopped on the long catty with the others for the tour.

The wine lands of Belheim Wine Estate was so beautiful. There were so many rows of different species of grapes, berries, and the whole nine. The tour guide even let us taste a few fruits from there ripest of trees.

After tasting their delicious fruits, we headed back to the main building for the wine and food tasting. The winery had a nice little setup of five tables. They were split up between white, red, and rose wine. And they also had some real high class dishes to match.

"Let's go taste the white wine first, Dre," Niniette stated. Then she grabbed my hand and dragged me over to the white wine table.

We first tasted some good Chenin Blanc and Lemon Parsley Roasted Chicken. Then we tried some Chardonnay Sur Lie and Creamy Mushroom Pasta.

"Niniette lets go taste some of the red wine before they drink it all," I stated.

I grabbed her hand and walked her over to the red wine table. First we tasted Grand Reserve and Duck with some Wild Mushroom Risotto. Then we tasted the Vera Cruz Pinotage with their Homemade Mushroom Burger and Rosemary Potato Wedges. Before we knew it, niggas had already killed the rest of the bottles. But it was all Gucci, we were already feeling nice off the wine we had already tasted.

"Niniette let's dip, our ride should be outside, anyway," I stated. I grabbed her hand and headed out the door.

The driver had actually just pulled up, as we headed out the entrance of winery. The driver hopped out, politely greeted us and opened our door. We slid in the shuttle, the driver shut our door, hopped in and pulled off back to resort. Forty-four minutes later and we pulled back up to the resort. We hopped out the shuttle, I walked over to the driver side and politely thanked the driver. Then I tipped him a fifty to send him on his way.

We walked around the hotel and onto the connecting rode that takes you all the way down to the spa island that was located at the heart of the resort. As we entered into the spa and approached the desk, we were politely greeted. After checking in at the desk, our masseuse came out and walked us over to spa treatment section. She told us to get undressed and lay face down, with our towels coving us. She then came back with some Baobab oil and an wooden rungu stick. Just before our masseuse started rubbing us down with the Baobab oil, Niniette reached and grabbed my hand. Then she turned over and mouthed the words "I love you" and then turned her head back down.

The masseuse really knew what she was doing with the baobab oil. After the rub down, she started to really dig into my muscles with the wooden rungu stick. Everything felt so calm, as the baobab oil started to sink into my skin. It was so weird, I could feel Niniette's spirit connecting stronger with mines, as she tighten the grip on my hand. At that moment I finally realized Niniette was the one. Thirty minutes later and the masseuse told us we could get dressed. Then she left us so we could get changed up. We then hopped out the massage bed and got dressed. Then we headed out of the massage hut, past the lobby of the spa and onto the rode of that connected to the rest of the resort.

A few minutes later and we entered into the hotel of the lobby. Then we made our way to the elevator and hopped on. We then rode it up to our level, hopped off and made our way down the hall then into our suite.

"Dre lets shower up before we had back out," Niniette stated.

I made my way to the bathroom and started up a shower. Niniette laid out the perfect fit for our journey up to Table Mountain. Then Niniette made her way into the bathroom and hopped into the shower with me.

Twenty minutes later and we hopped out of the shower. Then we head into the master bedroom to get dressed. We then make our way out the suite and down the hall to the elevator. We rode it down to the lobby and headed out the door just as our shuttle just pulled up. The driver hopped out, politely greeted us and opened our door. Then we slid in and closed the door. He then hopped back in and pulled off onto Table Mountain. Eighteen minutes and we pull up to the base of Table Mountain.

"We're going to take the funicular up to the top of Table mountain," I stated to Niniette. Then we slid out the shuttle and made our way to the funicular.

Damn this feeling is amazing, I can't believe I'm actually about to do this, I thought to myself as the funicular took us slowly up Table Mountain.

Finally the funicular brought us all the 3,560 ft. mountain side. We hopped off the funicular and walked over to the edge of Table mountain.

"Dre, this is beautiful," she stated as daylight shortly faded into nightfall. "I can see all of the Robben island from up here."

"Niniette?!" I stated as she turned around only to find me sitting on one knee holding a velvet creme ring box in my hand that had a very shiny and beautiful Amethyst ring with diamonds wrapped around it.

"Dre, what the," she said with excitement while in a state of shock.

"Niniette Jackson will you marry me?" I questioned.

"Dre…" she said as tears started to fall.

www.ingramcontent.com/pod-product-compliance
Lightning Source LLC
Chambersburg PA
CBHW082047220626
47052CB00007B/1246